HERGÉ
★
THE ADVENTURES OF
TINTIN
★

LAND
OF
BLACK GOLD

الذَّهَب الأَسْوَدْ

LITTLE, BROWN AND COMPANY
New York   Boston

Little, Brown and Company

Hachette Book Group
237 Park Avenue, New York, NY 10017
Visit our website at www.lb-kids.com

Little, Brown and company is a division of Hachette Book Group, Inc.
The Little, Brown name and logo are trademarks of Hachette Book Group, Inc.

The publisher is not responsible for websites (or their content) that are not owned by the publisher.

First U.S. Edition: September 1975
ISBN 978-0316-35844-6

Library of Congress card catalog no. 75-7896
30 29 28 27 26 25 24 23

Published pursuant to agreement with Casterman, Belgium.
Not for sale in the British Commonwealth.
Manufactured in China.

LAND OF BLACK GOLD

الذهب الأسود

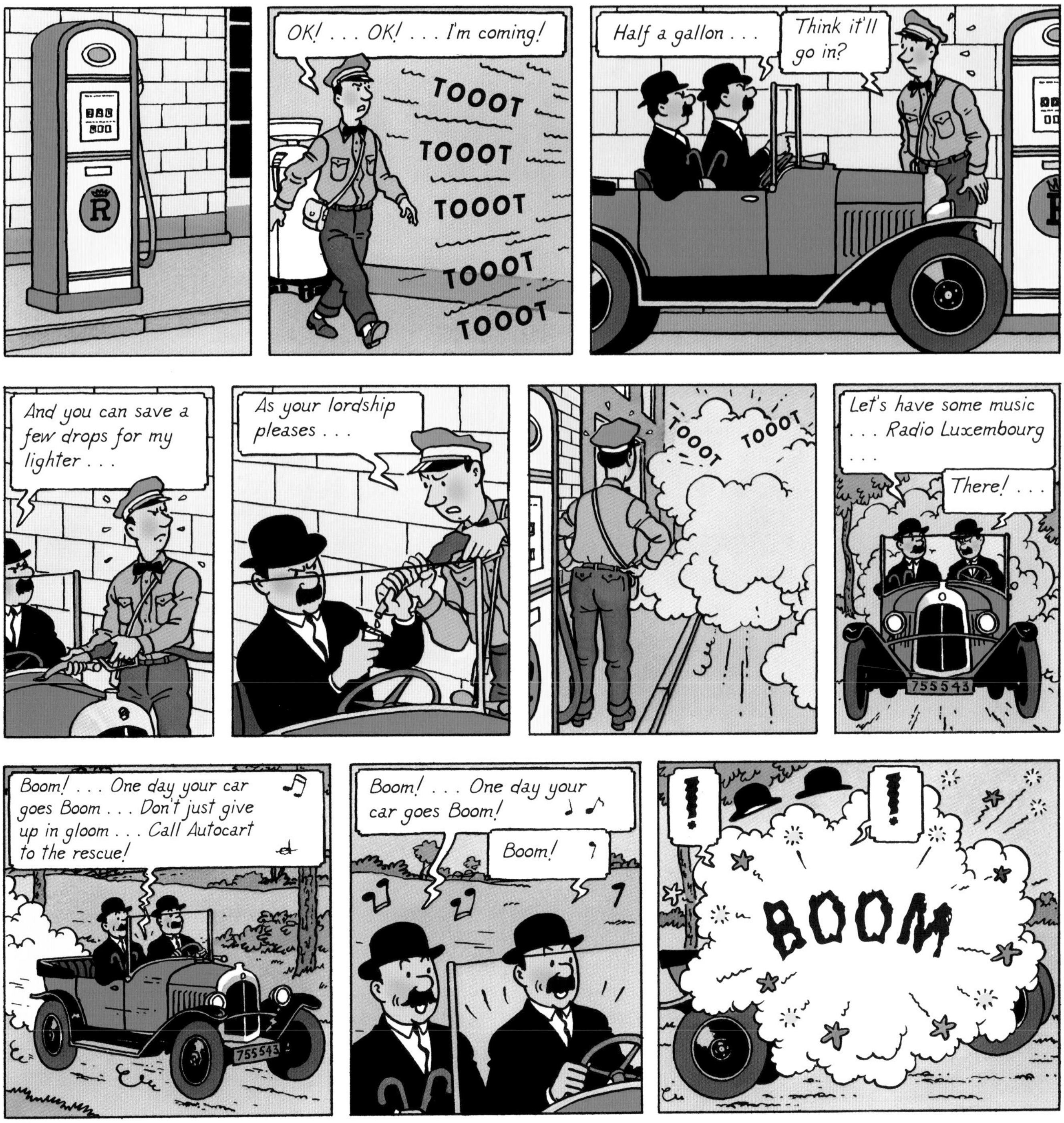
OK! . . . OK! . . . I'm coming!
TOOOT
TOOOT
TOOOT
TOOOT
TOOOT
Half a gallon . . .
Think it'll go in?
And you can save a few drops for my lighter . . .
As your lordship pleases . . .
TOOOT
TOOOT
Let's have some music . . . Radio Luxembourg . . .
There! . . .
Boom! . . . One day your car goes Boom . . . Don't just give up in gloom . . . Call Autocart to the rescue!
Boom! . . . One day your car goes Boom!
Boom!
!
!
BOOM

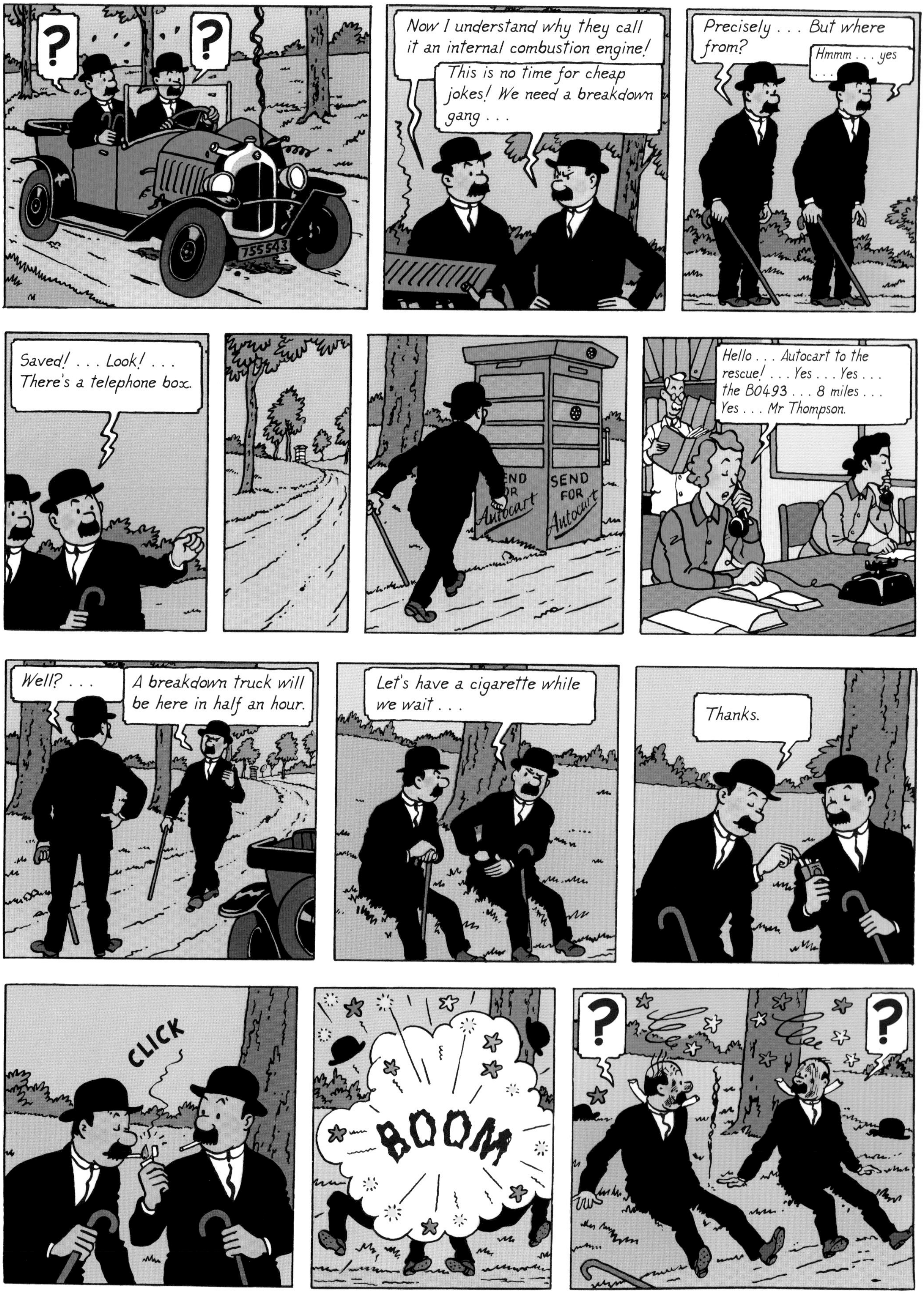
?
?
Now I understand why they call it an internal combustion engine!
This is no time for cheap jokes! We need a breakdown gang . . .
Precisely . . . But where from?
Hmmm . . . yes . . .
Saved! . . . Look! . . . There's a telephone box.
SEND FOR Autocart
SEND FOR Autocart
Hello . . . Autocart to the rescue! . . . Yes . . . Yes . . . the B0493 . . . 8 miles . . . Yes . . . Mr Thompson.
Well? . . .
A breakdown truck will be here in half an hour.
Let's have a cigarette while we wait . . .
Thanks.
CLICK
BOOM
?
?

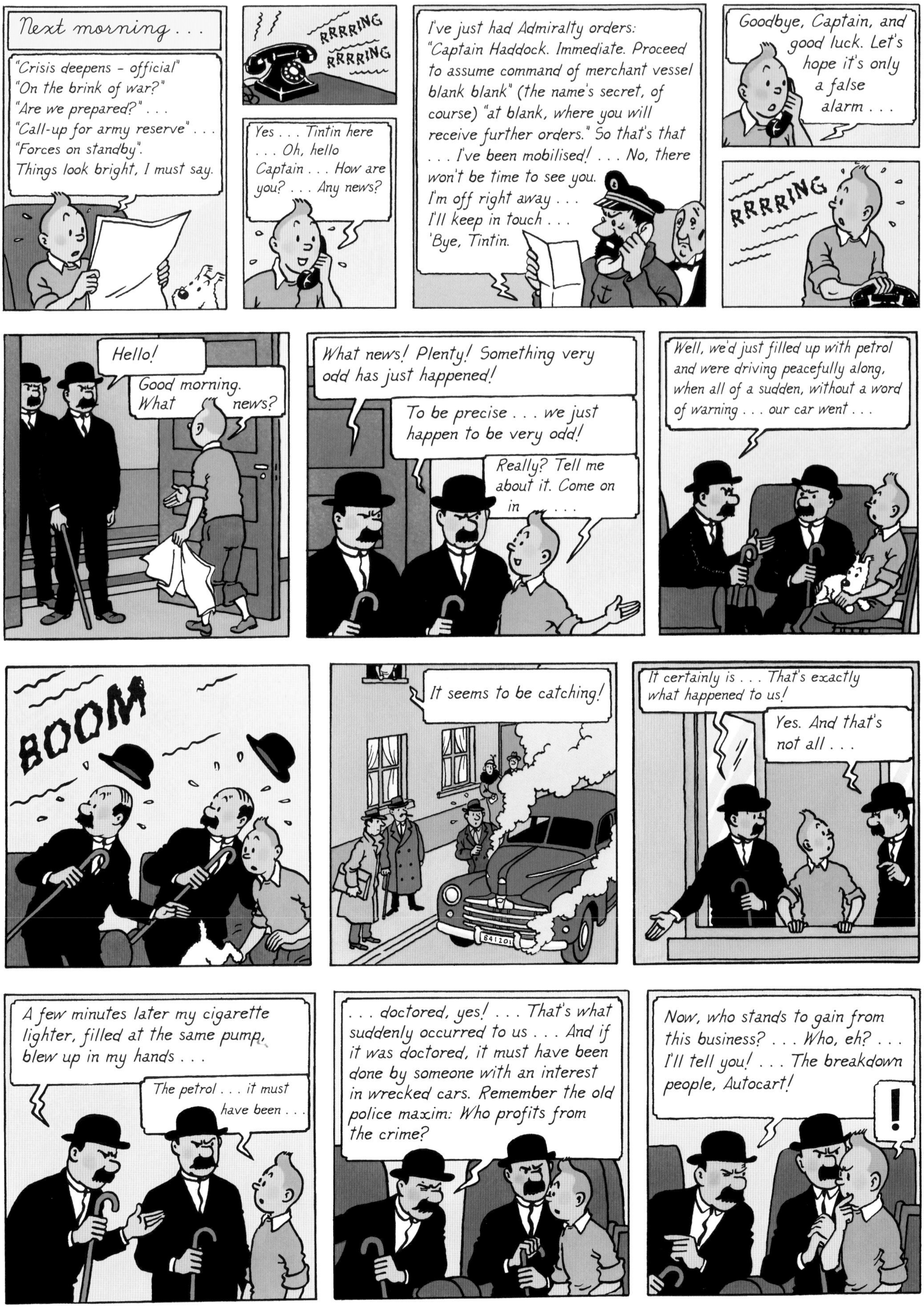
Next morning . . .
"Crisis deepens – official" "On the brink of war?" "Are we prepared?" . . . "Call-up for army reserve" . . . "Forces on standby". Things look bright, I must say.
RRRRING RRRRING
Yes . . . Tintin here . . . Oh, hello Captain . . . How are you? . . . Any news?
I've just had Admiralty orders: "Captain Haddock. Immediate. Proceed to assume command of merchant vessel blank blank" (the name's secret, of course) "at blank, where you will receive further orders." So that's that . . . I've been mobilised! . . . No, there won't be time to see you. I'm off right away . . . I'll keep in touch . . . 'Bye, Tintin.
Goodbye, Captain, and good luck. Let's hope it's only a false alarm . . .
RRRRING
Hello!
Good morning. What news?
What news! Plenty! Something very odd has just happened!
To be precise . . . we just happen to be very odd!
Really? Tell me about it. Come on in . . .
Well, we'd just filled up with petrol and were driving peacefully along, when all of a sudden, without a word of warning . . . our car went . . .
BOOM
It seems to be catching!
It certainly is . . . That's exactly what happened to us!
Yes. And that's not all . . .
A few minutes later my cigarette lighter, filled at the same pump, blew up in my hands . . .
The petrol . . . it must have been . . .
. . . doctored, yes! . . . That's what suddenly occurred to us . . . And if it was doctored, it must have been done by someone with an interest in wrecked cars. Remember the old police maxim: Who profits from the crime?
Now, who stands to gain from this business? . . . Who, eh? . . . I'll tell you! . . . The breakdown people, Autocart!
!

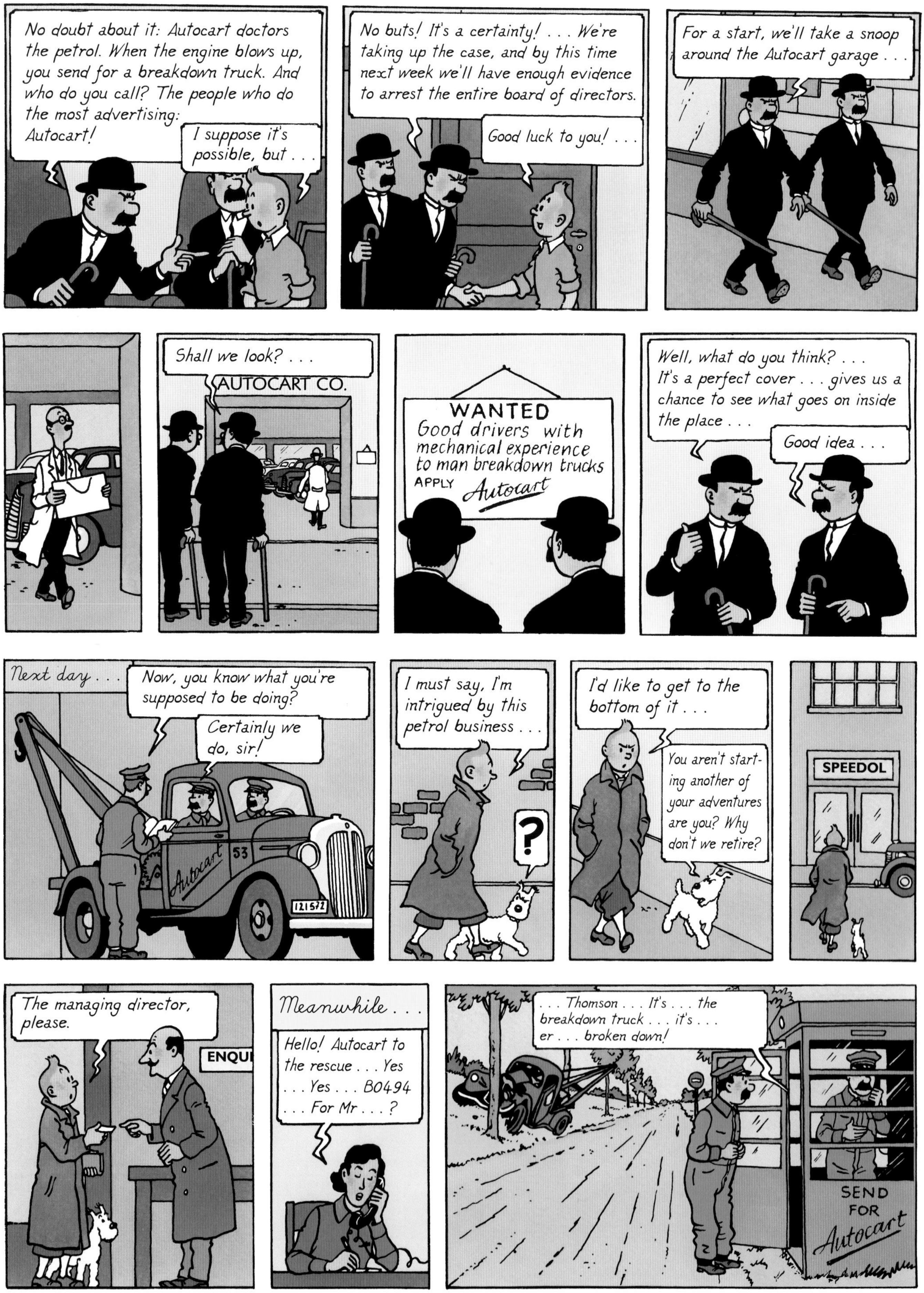
No doubt about it: Autocart doctors the petrol. When the engine blows up, you send for a breakdown truck. And who do you call? The people who do the most advertising: Autocart!
I suppose it's possible, but . . .
No buts! It's a certainty! . . . We're taking up the case, and by this time next week we'll have enough evidence to arrest the entire board of directors.
Good luck to you! . . .
For a start, we'll take a snoop around the Autocart garage . . .
Shall we look? . . .
AUTOCART CO.
WANTED
Good drivers with mechanical experience to man breakdown trucks
APPLY Autocart
Well, what do you think? . . . It's a perfect cover . . . gives us a chance to see what goes on inside the place . . .
Good idea . . .
Next day . . .
Now, you know what you're supposed to be doing?
Certainly we do, sir!
Autocart
53
121572
I must say, I'm intrigued by this petrol business . . .
?
I'd like to get to the bottom of it . . .
You aren't starting another of your adventures are you? Why don't we retire?
SPEEDOL
The managing director, please.
ENQU
Meanwhile . . .
Hello! Autocart to the rescue . . . Yes . . . Yes . . . B0494 . . . For Mr . . . ?
. . . Thomson . . . It's . . . the breakdown truck . . . it's . . . er . . . broken down!
SEND FOR Autocart

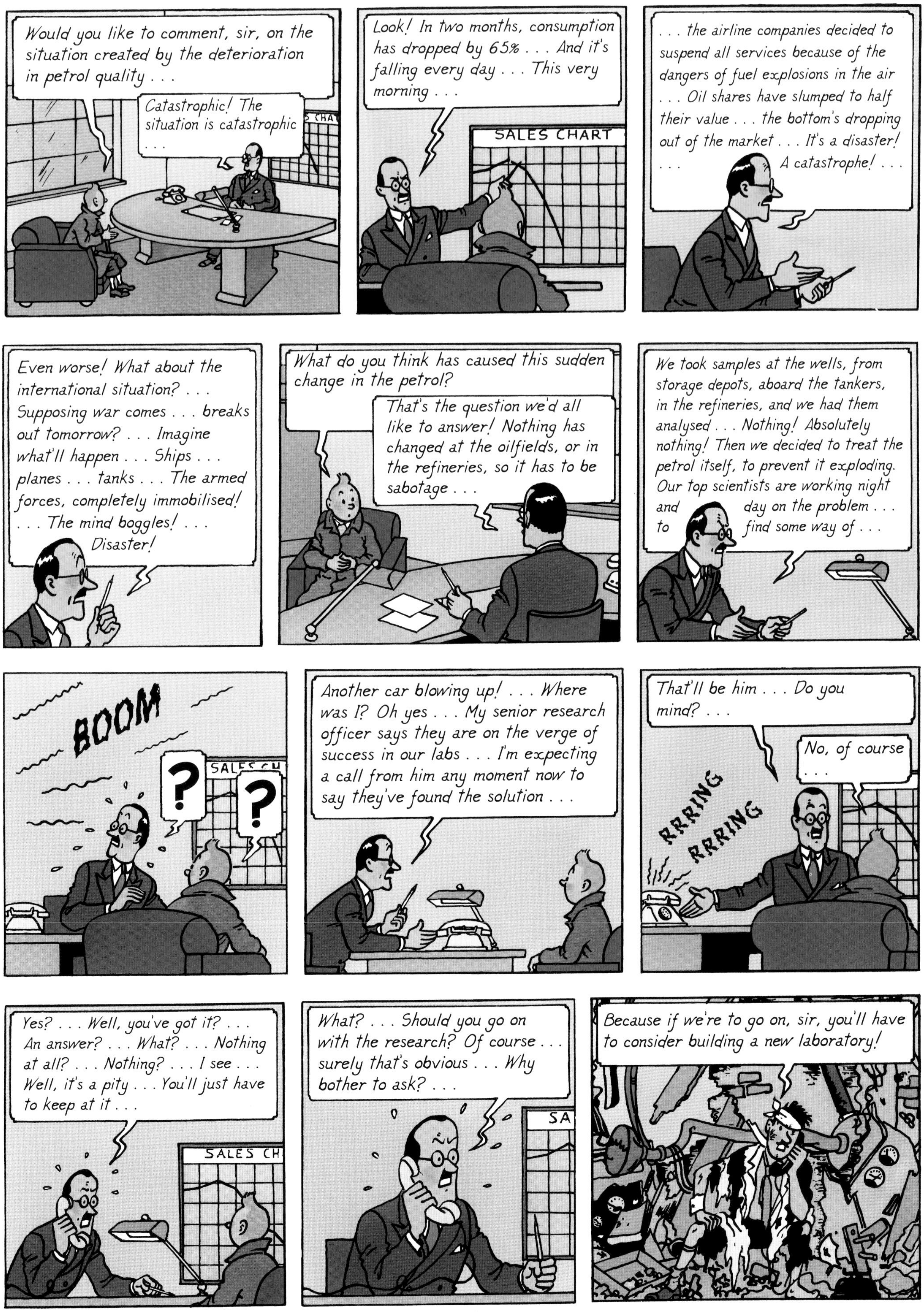
Would you like to comment, sir, on the situation created by the deterioration in petrol quality . . .
Catastrophic! The situation is catastrophic . . .
Look! In two months, consumption has dropped by 65% . . . And it's falling every day . . . This very morning . . .
SALES CHART
. . . the airline companies decided to suspend all services because of the dangers of fuel explosions in the air . . . Oil shares have slumped to half their value . . . the bottom's dropping out of the market . . . It's a disaster! . . . A catastrophe! . . .
Even worse! What about the international situation? . . . Supposing war comes . . . breaks out tomorrow? . . . Imagine what'll happen . . . Ships . . . planes . . . tanks . . . The armed forces, completely immobilised! . . . The mind boggles! . . . Disaster!
What do you think has caused this sudden change in the petrol?
That's the question we'd all like to answer! Nothing has changed at the oilfields, or in the refineries, so it has to be sabotage . . .
We took samples at the wells, from storage depots, aboard the tankers, in the refineries, and we had them analysed . . . Nothing! Absolutely nothing! Then we decided to treat the petrol itself, to prevent it exploding. Our top scientists are working night and day on the problem . . . to find some way of . . .
BOOM
?
?
Another car blowing up! . . . Where was I? Oh yes . . . My senior research officer says they are on the verge of success in our labs . . . I'm expecting a call from him any moment now to say they've found the solution . . .
That'll be him . . . Do you mind? . . .
No, of course . . .
RRRING
RRRING
Yes? . . . Well, you've got it? . . . An answer? . . . What? . . . Nothing at all? . . . Nothing? . . . I see . . . Well, it's a pity . . . You'll just have to keep at it . . .
What? . . . Should you go on with the research? Of course . . . surely that's obvious . . . Why bother to ask? . . .
Because if we're to go on, sir, you'll have to consider building a new laboratory!

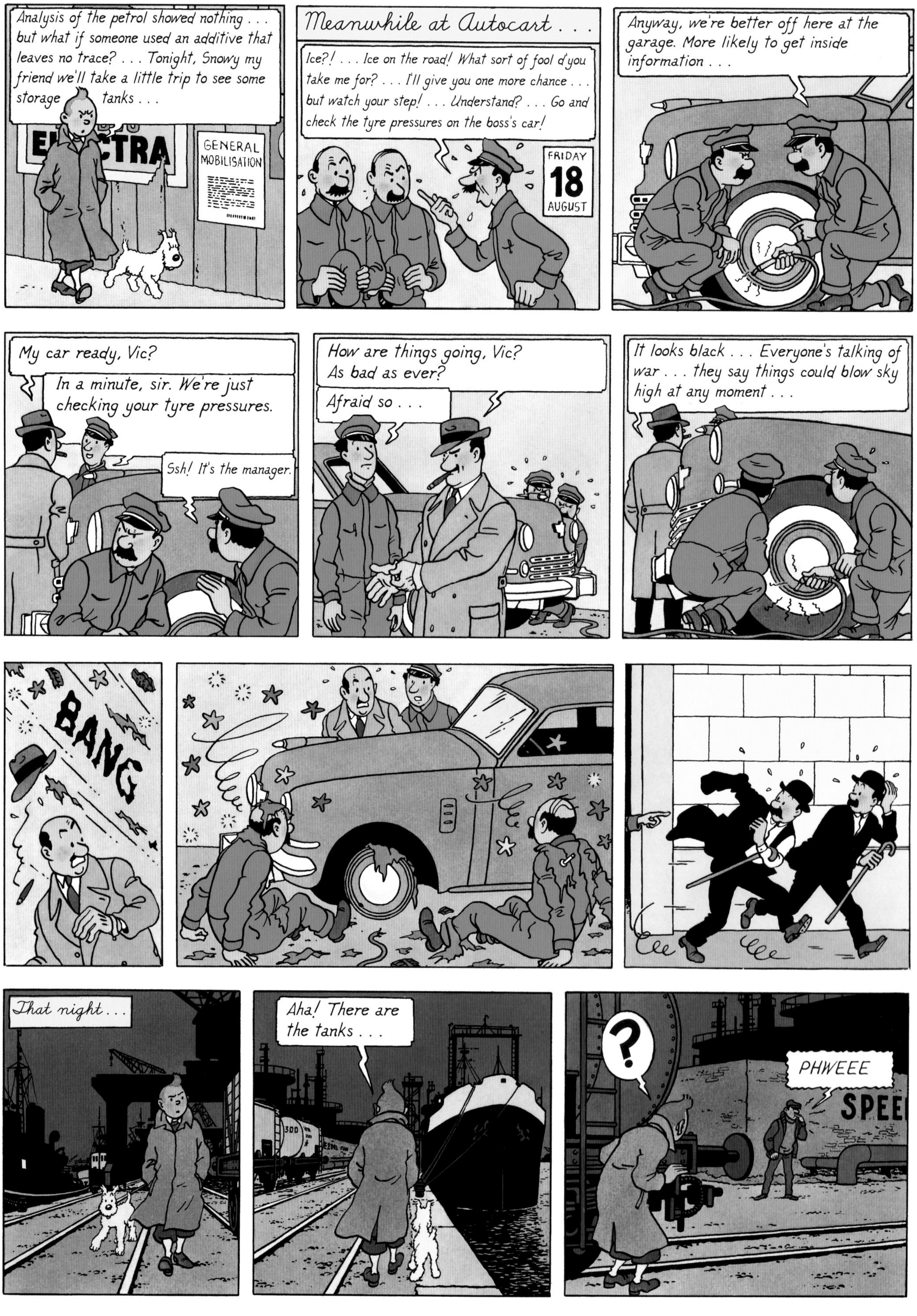

Analysis of the petrol showed nothing . . . but what if someone used an additive that leaves no trace? . . . Tonight, Snowy my friend we'll take a little trip to see some storage tanks . . .
ELECTRA
GENERAL MOBILISATION
Meanwhile at Autocart . . .
Ice?! . . . Ice on the road! What sort of fool d'you take me for? . . . I'll give you one more chance . . . but watch your step! . . . Understand? . . . Go and check the tyre pressures on the boss's car!
FRIDAY 18 AUGUST
Anyway, we're better off here at the garage. More likely to get inside information . . .
My car ready, Vic?
In a minute, sir. We're just checking your tyre pressures.
Ssh! It's the manager.
How are things going, Vic? As bad as ever?
Afraid so . . .
It looks black . . . Everyone's talking of war . . . they say things could blow sky high at any moment . . .
BANG
That night . . .
Aha! There are the tanks . . .
?
PHWEEE
SPEE

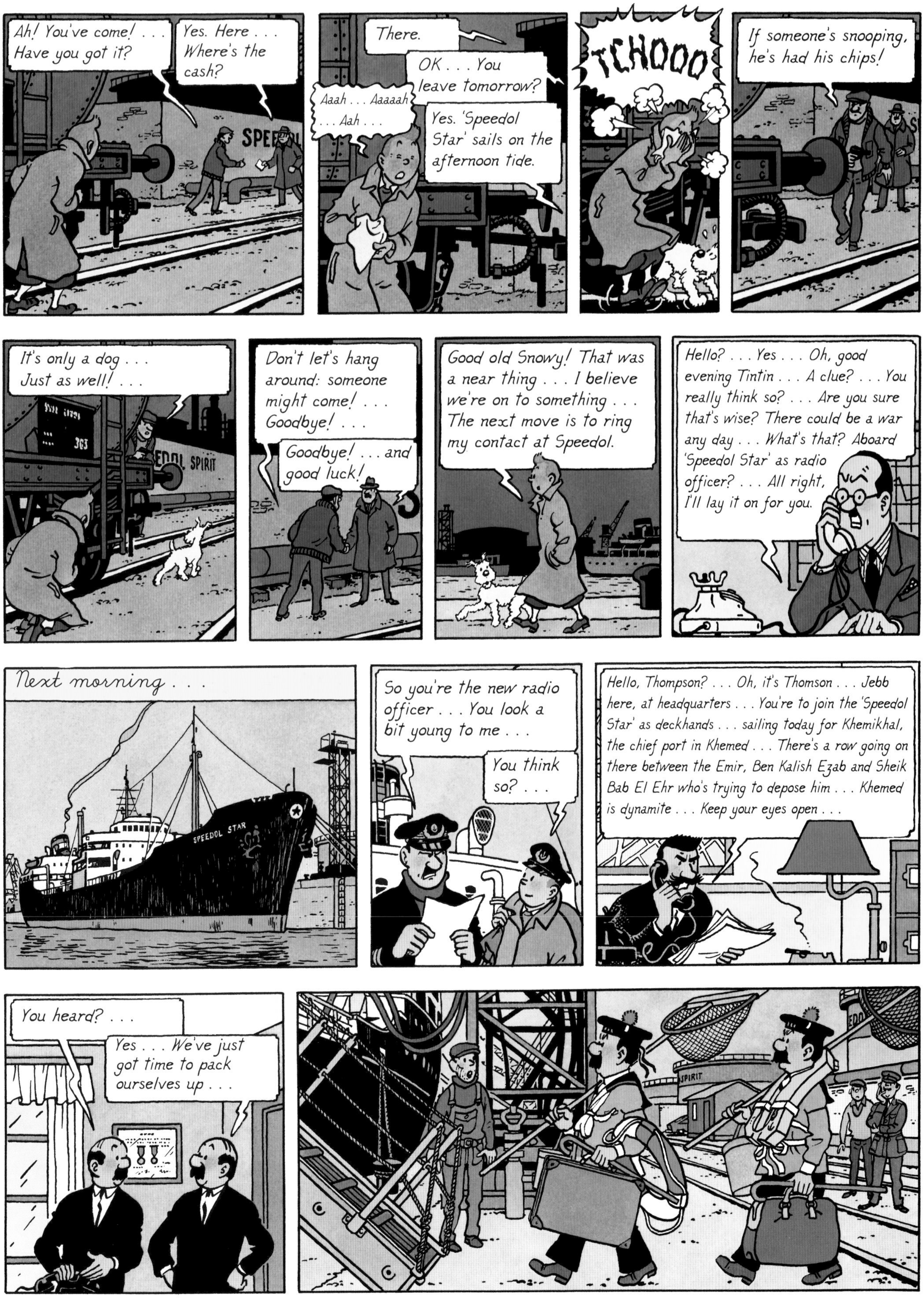
Ah! You've come! . . . Have you got it?
Yes. Here . . . Where's the cash?
SPEE
There.
OK . . . You leave tomorrow?
Aaah . . . Aaaaah . . . Aah . . .
Yes. 'Speedol Star' sails on the afternoon tide.
TCHOOO
If someone's snooping, he's had his chips!
It's only a dog . . . Just as well! . . .
SPEEDOL SPIRIT
Don't let's hang around: someone might come! . . . Goodbye! . . .
Goodbye! . . . and good luck!
Good old Snowy! That was a near thing . . . I believe we're on to something . . . The next move is to ring my contact at Speedol.
Hello? . . . Yes . . . Oh, good evening Tintin . . . A clue? . . . You really think so? . . . Are you sure that's wise? There could be a war any day . . . What's that? Aboard 'Speedol Star' as radio officer? . . . All right, I'll lay it on for you.
Next morning . . .
SPEEDOL STAR
So you're the new radio officer . . . You look a bit young to me . . .
You think so? . . .
Hello, Thompson? . . . Oh, it's Thomson . . . Jebb here, at headquarters . . . You're to join the 'Speedol Star' as deckhands . . . sailing today for Khemikhal, the chief port in Khemed . . . There's a row going on there between the Emir, Ben Kalish Ezab and Sheik Bab El Ehr who's trying to depose him . . . Khemed is dynamite . . . Keep your eyes open . . .
You heard? . . .
Yes . . . We've just got time to pack ourselves up . . .
SPIRIT

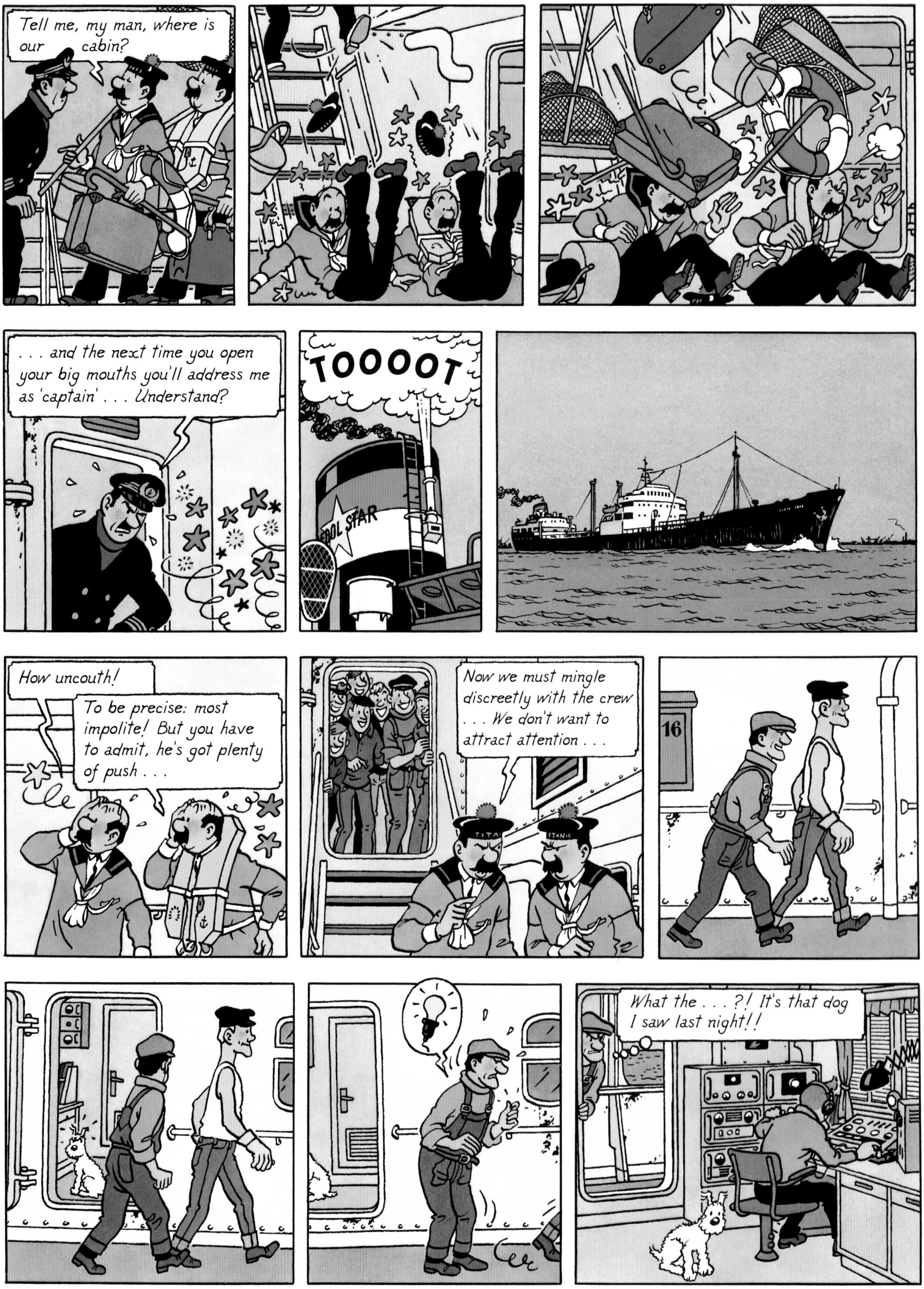
Tell me, my man, where is our cabin?
. . . and the next time you open your big mouths you'll address me as 'captain' . . . Understand?
TOOOOT
How uncouth!
To be precise: most impolite! But you have to admit, he's got plenty of push . . .
Now we must mingle discreetly with the crew . . . We don't want to attract attention . . .
16
What the . . . ?! It's that dog I saw last night!!

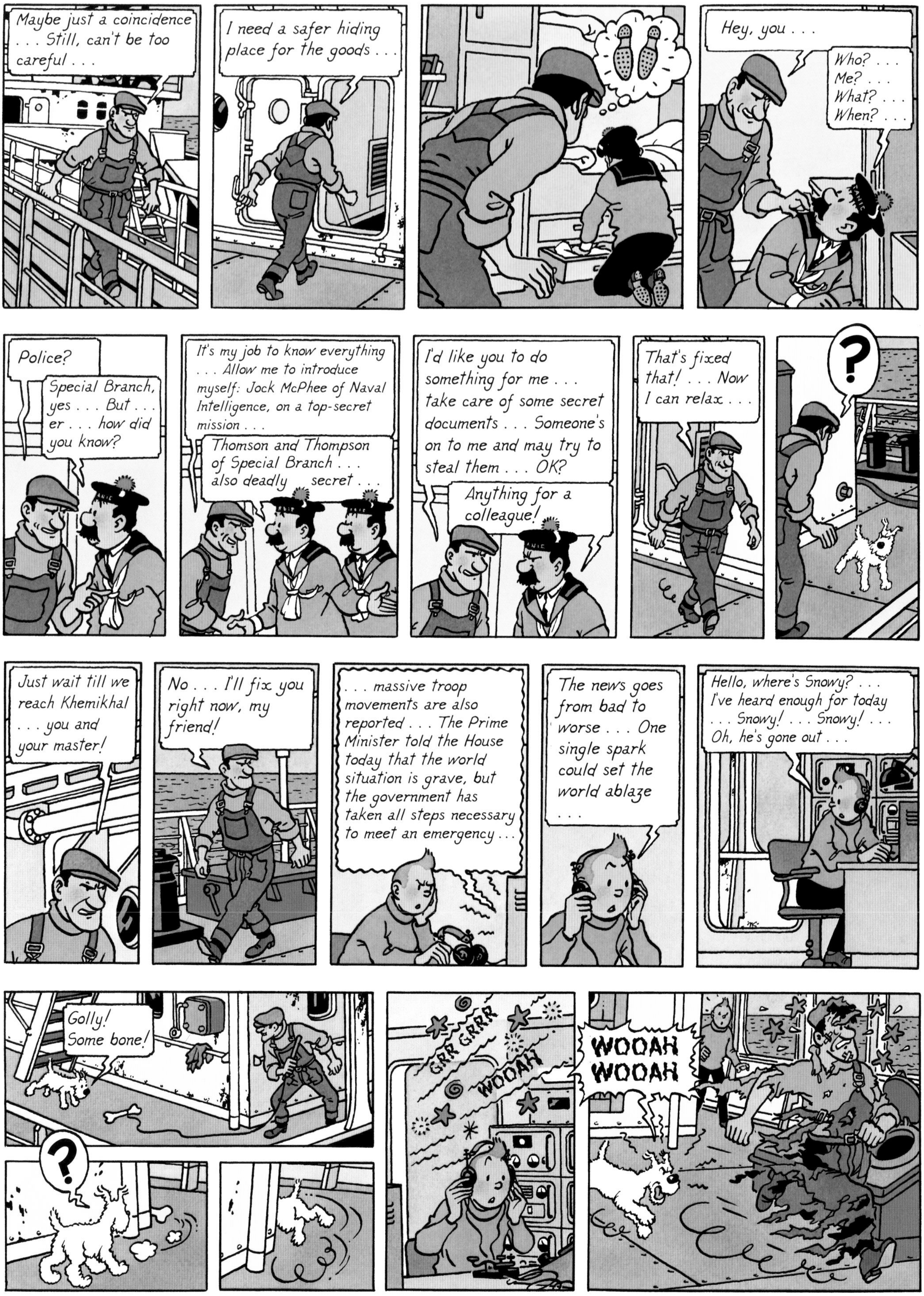
Maybe just a coincidence . . . Still, can't be too careful . . .
I need a safer hiding place for the goods . . .
Hey, you . . .
Who? . . . Me? . . . What? . . . When? . . .
Police?
Special Branch, yes . . . But . . . er . . . how did you know?
It's my job to know everything . . . Allow me to introduce myself: Jock McPhee of Naval Intelligence, on a top-secret mission . . .
Thomson and Thompson of Special Branch . . . also deadly secret . . .
I'd like you to do something for me . . . take care of some secret documents . . . Someone's on to me and may try to steal them . . . OK?
Anything for a colleague!
That's fixed that! . . . Now I can relax . . .
?
Just wait till we reach Khemikhal . . . you and your master!
No . . . I'll fix you right now, my friend!
. . . massive troop movements are also reported . . . The Prime Minister told the House today that the world situation is grave, but the government has taken all steps necessary to meet an emergency . . .
The news goes from bad to worse . . . One single spark could set the world ablaze . . .
Hello, where's Snowy? . . . I've heard enough for today . . . Snowy! . . . Snowy! . . . Oh, he's gone out . . .
Golly! Some bone!
?
GRR GRRR
WOOAH
WOOAH WOOAH

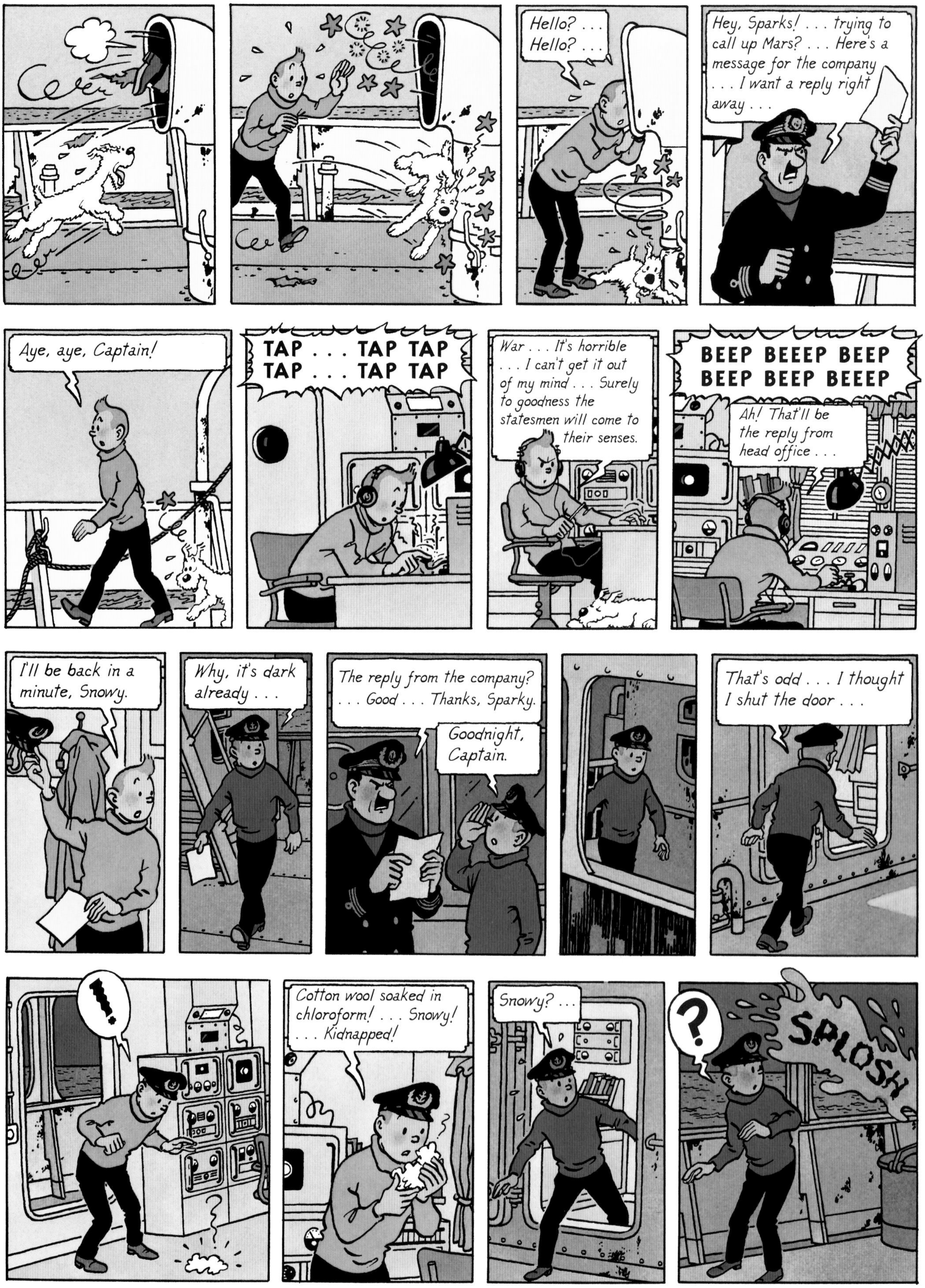
Hello? . . .
Hello? . . .
Hey, Sparks! . . . trying to call up Mars? . . . Here's a message for the company . . . I want a reply right away . . .
Aye, aye, Captain!
TAP . . . TAP TAP
TAP . . . TAP TAP
War . . . It's horrible . . . I can't get it out of my mind . . . Surely to goodness the statesmen will come to their senses.
BEEP BEEEP BEEP
BEEP BEEP BEEEP
Ah! That'll be the reply from head office . . .
I'll be back in a minute, Snowy.
Why, it's dark already . . .
The reply from the company? . . . Good . . . Thanks, Sparky.
Goodnight, Captain.
That's odd . . . I thought I shut the door . . .
!
Cotton wool soaked in chloroform! . . . Snowy! . . . Kidnapped!
Snowy? . . .
?
SPLOSH

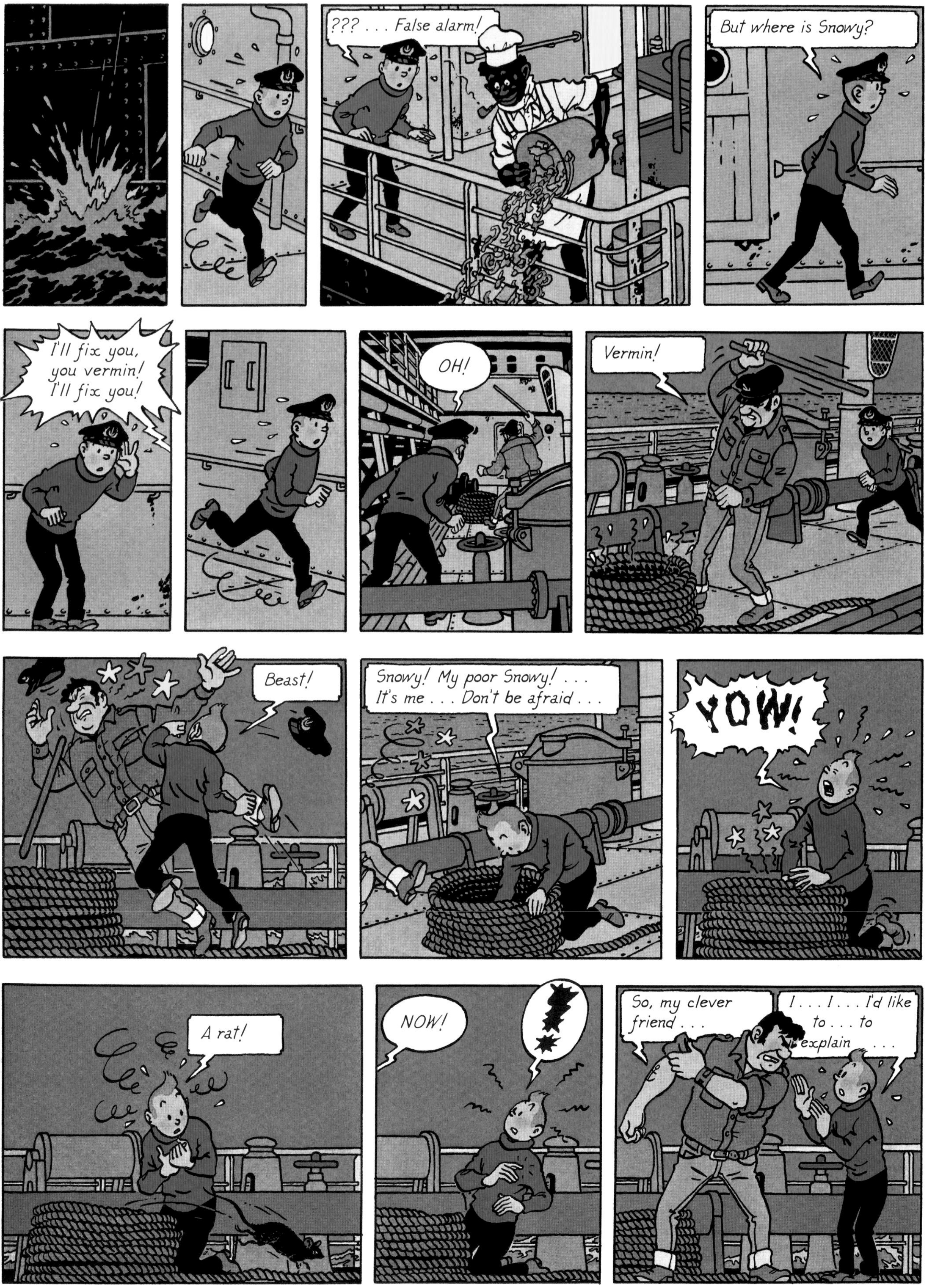
??? . . . False alarm!
But where is Snowy?
I'll fix you, you vermin! I'll fix you!
OH!
Vermin!
Beast!
Snowy! My poor Snowy! . . . It's me . . . Don't be afraid . . .
YOW!
A rat!
NOW!
So, my clever friend . . .
I . . . I . . . I'd like to . . . to explain . . .

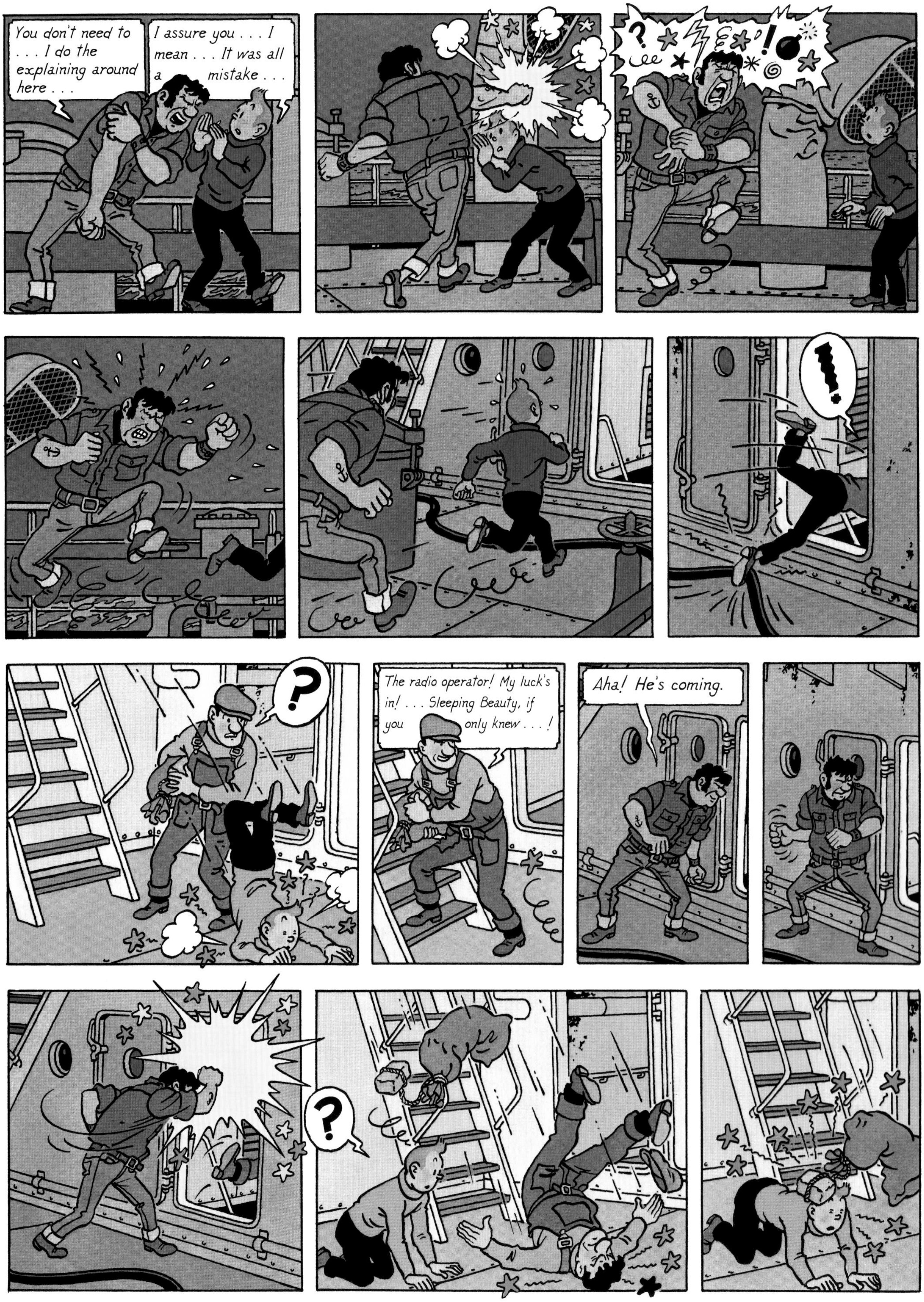

You don't need to . . . I do the explaining around here . . .
I assure you . . . I mean . . . It was all a mistake . . .
The radio operator! My luck's in! . . . Sleeping Beauty, if you only knew . . . !
Aha! He's coming.

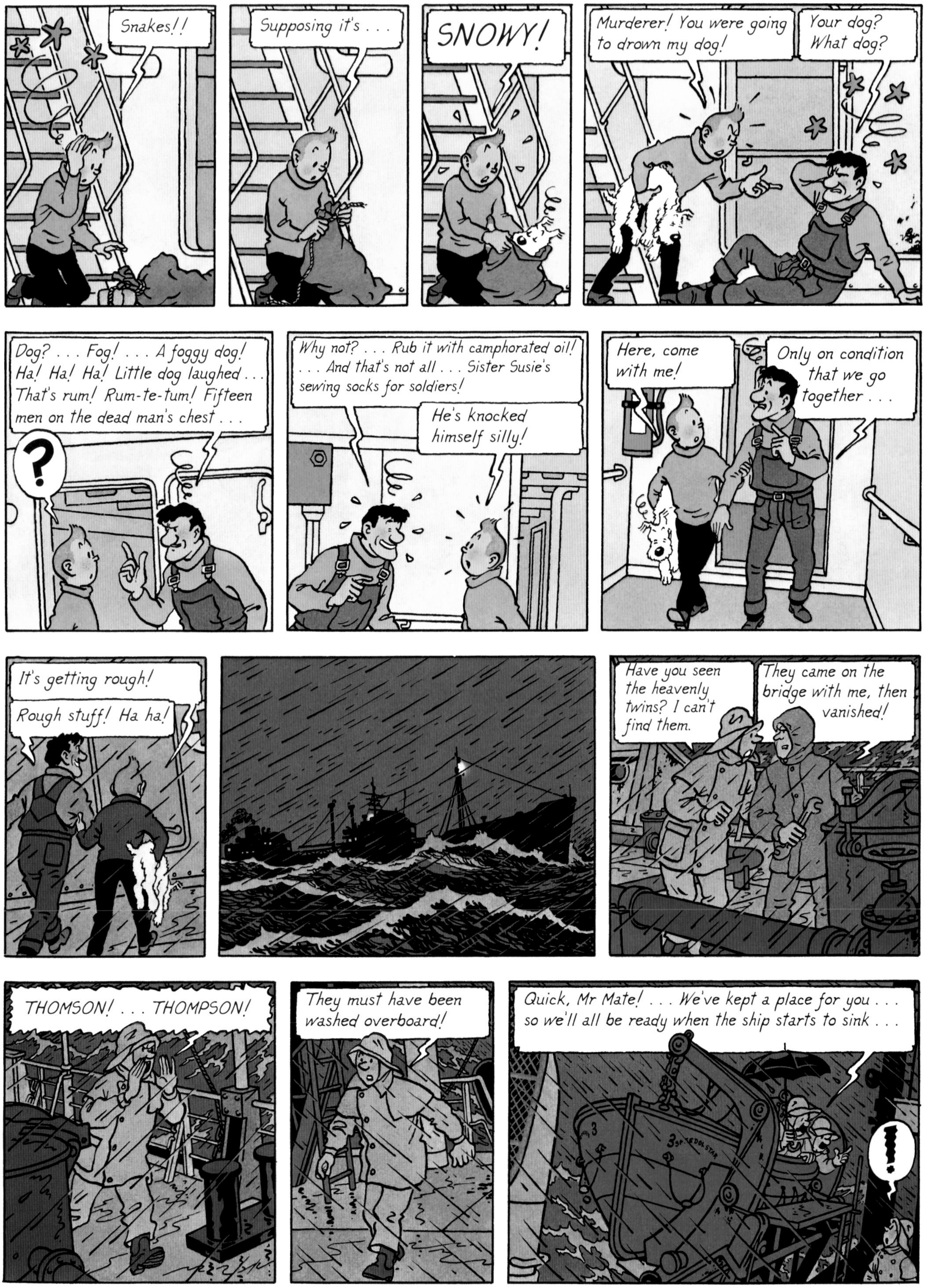

Snakes!!
Supposing it's . . .
SNOWY!
Murderer! You were going to drown my dog!
Your dog? What dog?
Dog? . . . Fog! . . . A foggy dog! Ha! Ha! Ha! Little dog laughed . . . That's rum! Rum-te-tum! Fifteen men on the dead man's chest . . .
?
Why not? . . . Rub it with camphorated oil! . . . And that's not all . . . Sister Susie's sewing socks for soldiers!
He's knocked himself silly!
Here, come with me!
Only on condition that we go together . . .
It's getting rough!
Rough stuff! Ha ha!
Have you seen the heavenly twins? I can't find them.
They came on the bridge with me, then vanished!
THOMSON! . . . THOMPSON!
They must have been washed overboard!
Quick, Mr Mate! . . . We've kept a place for you . . . so we'll all be ready when the ship starts to sink . . .

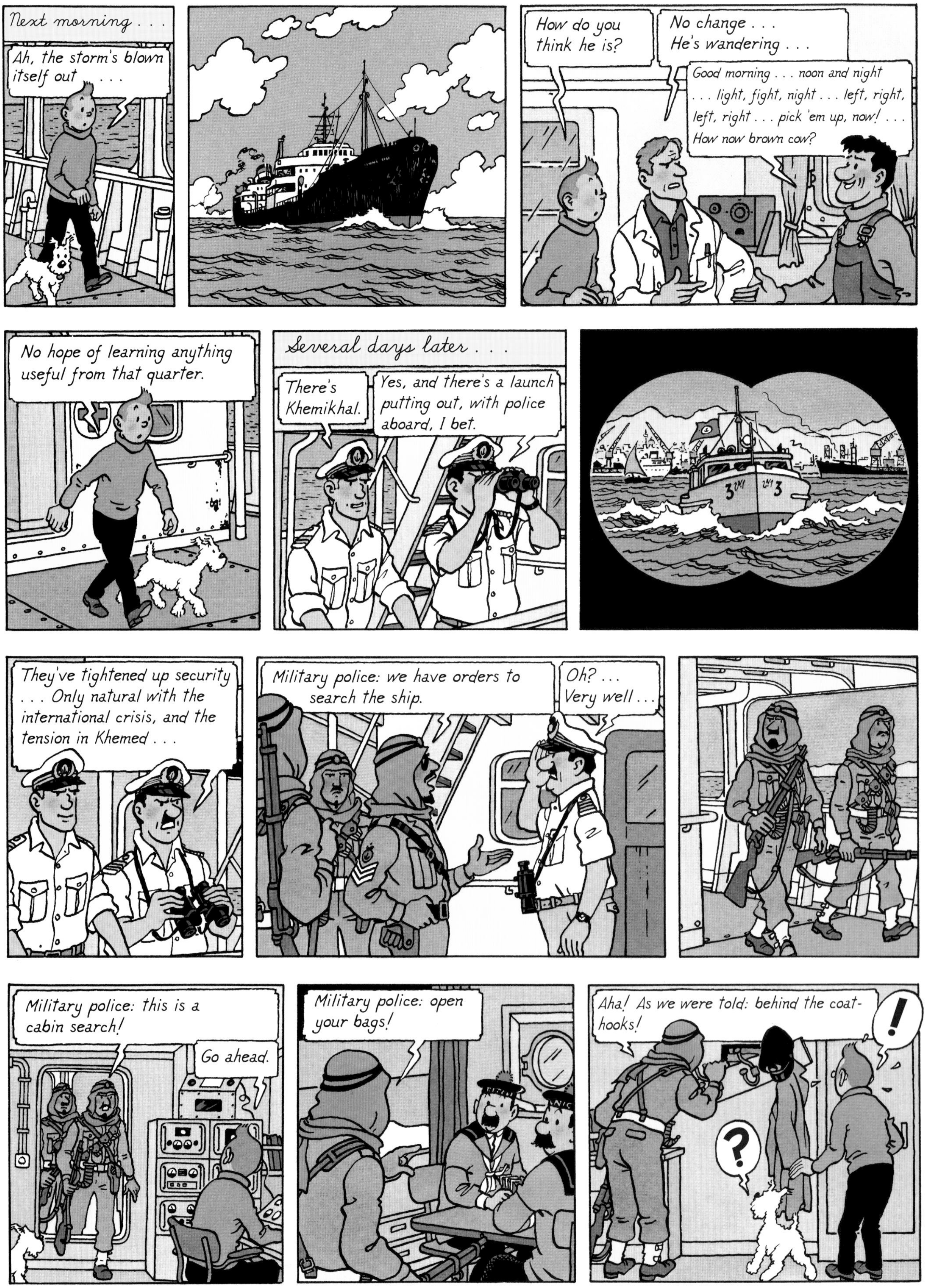
Next morning . . .
Ah, the storm's blown itself out . . .
How do you think he is?
No change . . . He's wandering . . .
Good morning . . . noon and night . . . light, fight, night . . . left, right, left, right . . . pick 'em up, now! . . . How now brown cow?
No hope of learning anything useful from that quarter.
Several days later . . .
There's Khemikhal.
Yes, and there's a launch putting out, with police aboard, I bet.
They've tightened up security . . . Only natural with the international crisis, and the tension in Khemed . . .
Military police: we have orders to search the ship.
Oh? . . . Very well . . .
Military police: this is a cabin search!
Go ahead.
Military police: open your bags!
Aha! As we were told: behind the coat-hooks!
!
?

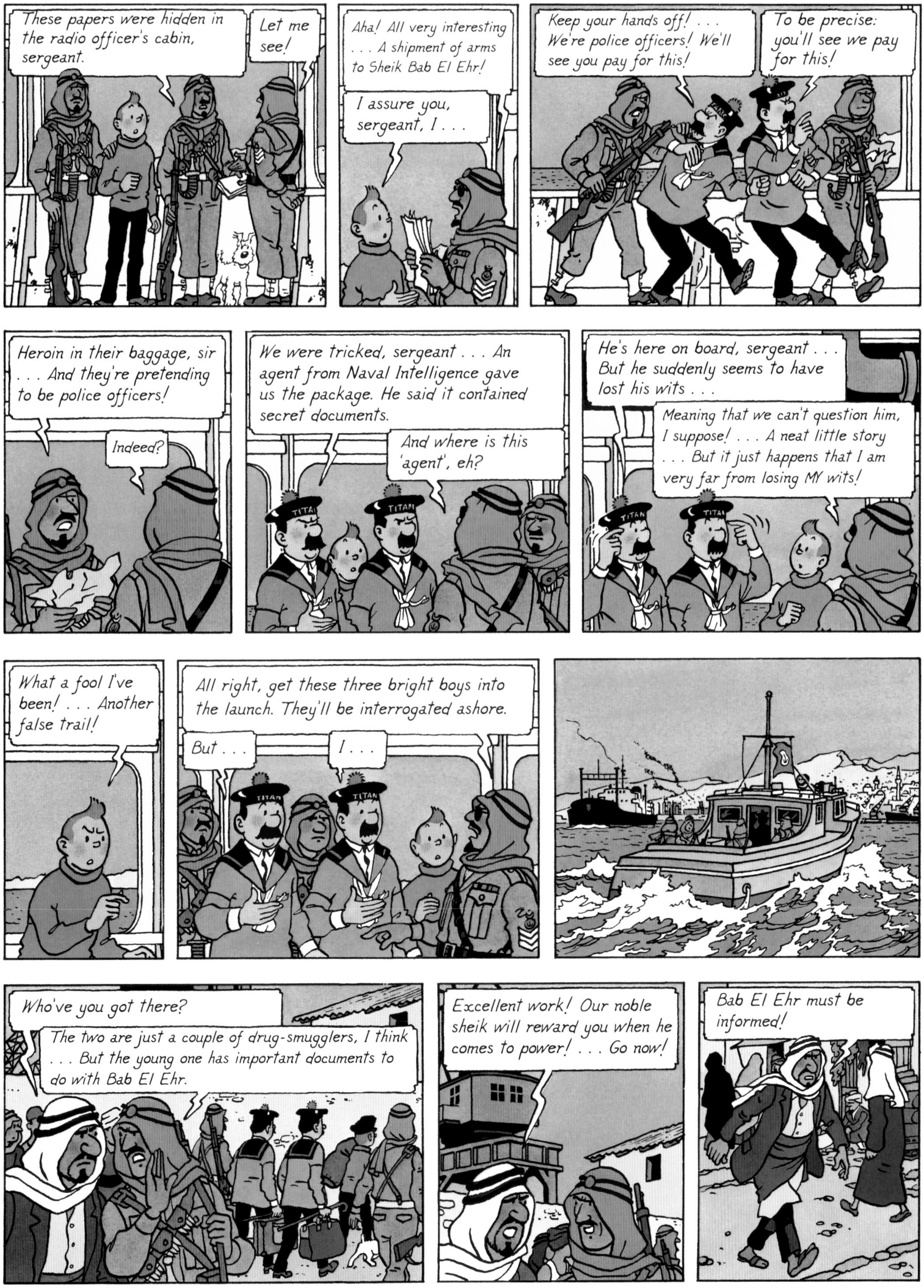
These papers were hidden in the radio officer's cabin, sergeant.
Let me see!
Aha! All very interesting . . . A shipment of arms to Sheik Bab El Ehr!
I assure you, sergeant, I . . .
Keep your hands off! . . . We're police officers! We'll see you pay for this!
To be precise: you'll see we pay for this!
Heroin in their baggage, sir . . . And they're pretending to be police officers!
Indeed?
We were tricked, sergeant . . . An agent from Naval Intelligence gave us the package. He said it contained secret documents.
And where is this 'agent', eh?
He's here on board, sergeant . . . But he suddenly seems to have lost his wits . . .
Meaning that we can't question him, I suppose! . . . A neat little story . . . But it just happens that I am very far from losing MY wits!
What a fool I've been! . . . Another false trail!
All right, get these three bright boys into the launch. They'll be interrogated ashore.
But . . .
I . . .
Who've you got there?
The two are just a couple of drug-smugglers, I think . . . But the young one has important documents to do with Bab El Ehr.
Excellent work! Our noble sheik will reward you when he comes to power! . . . Go now!
Bab El Ehr must be informed!

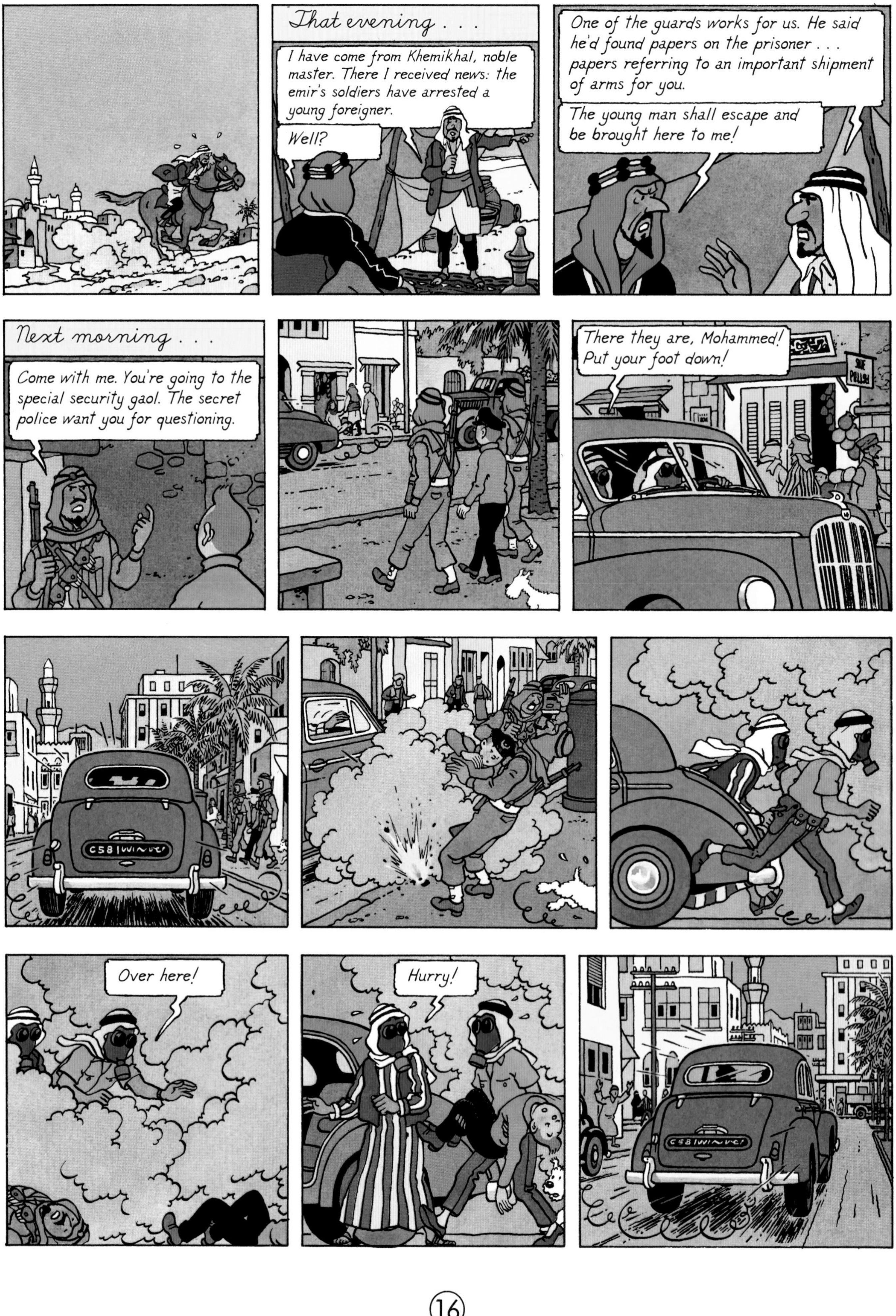
That evening . . .
I have come from Khemikhal, noble master. There I received news: the emir's soldiers have arrested a young foreigner.
Well?
One of the guards works for us. He said he'd found papers on the prisoner . . . papers referring to an important shipment of arms for you.
The young man shall escape and be brought here to me!
Next morning . . .
Come with me. You're going to the special security gaol. The secret police want you for questioning.
There they are, Mohammed! Put your foot down!
Over here!
Hurry!

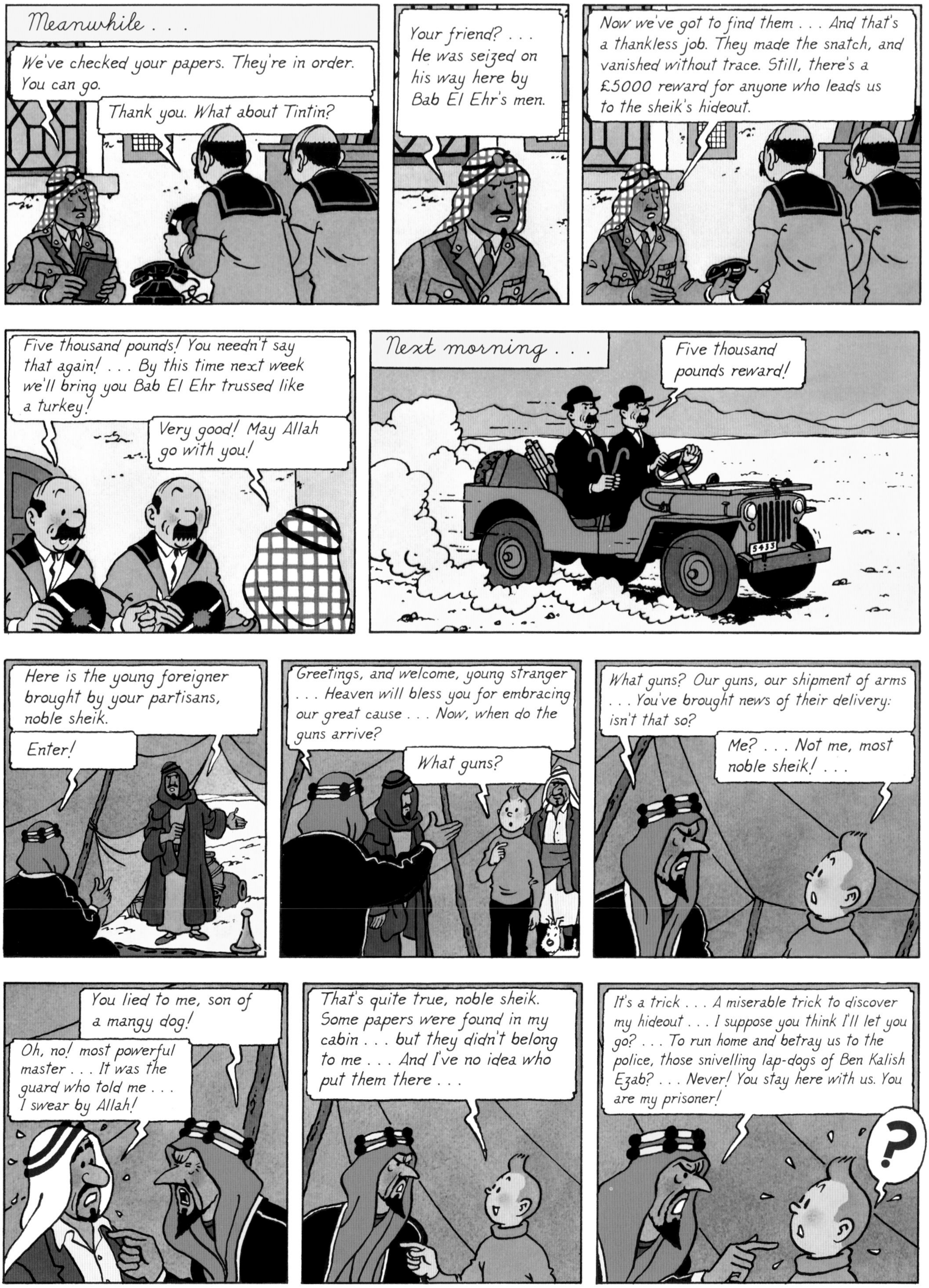
Meanwhile . . .
We've checked your papers. They're in order. You can go.
Thank you. What about Tintin?
Your friend? . . . He was seized on his way here by Bab El Ehr's men.
Now we've got to find them . . . And that's a thankless job. They made the snatch, and vanished without trace. Still, there's a £5000 reward for anyone who leads us to the sheik's hideout.
Five thousand pounds! You needn't say that again! . . . By this time next week we'll bring you Bab El Ehr trussed like a turkey!
Very good! May Allah go with you!
Next morning . . .
Five thousand pounds reward!
Here is the young foreigner brought by your partisans, noble sheik.
Enter!
Greetings, and welcome, young stranger . . . Heaven will bless you for embracing our great cause . . . Now, when do the guns arrive?
What guns?
What guns? Our guns, our shipment of arms . . . You've brought news of their delivery: isn't that so?
Me? . . . Not me, most noble sheik! . . .
You lied to me, son of a mangy dog!
Oh, no! most powerful master . . . It was the guard who told me . . . I swear by Allah!
That's quite true, noble sheik. Some papers were found in my cabin . . . but they didn't belong to me . . . And I've no idea who put them there . . .
It's a trick . . . A miserable trick to discover my hideout . . . I suppose you think I'll let you go? . . . To run home and betray us to the police, those snivelling lap-dogs of Ben Kalish Ezab? . . . Never! You stay here with us. You are my prisoner!
?

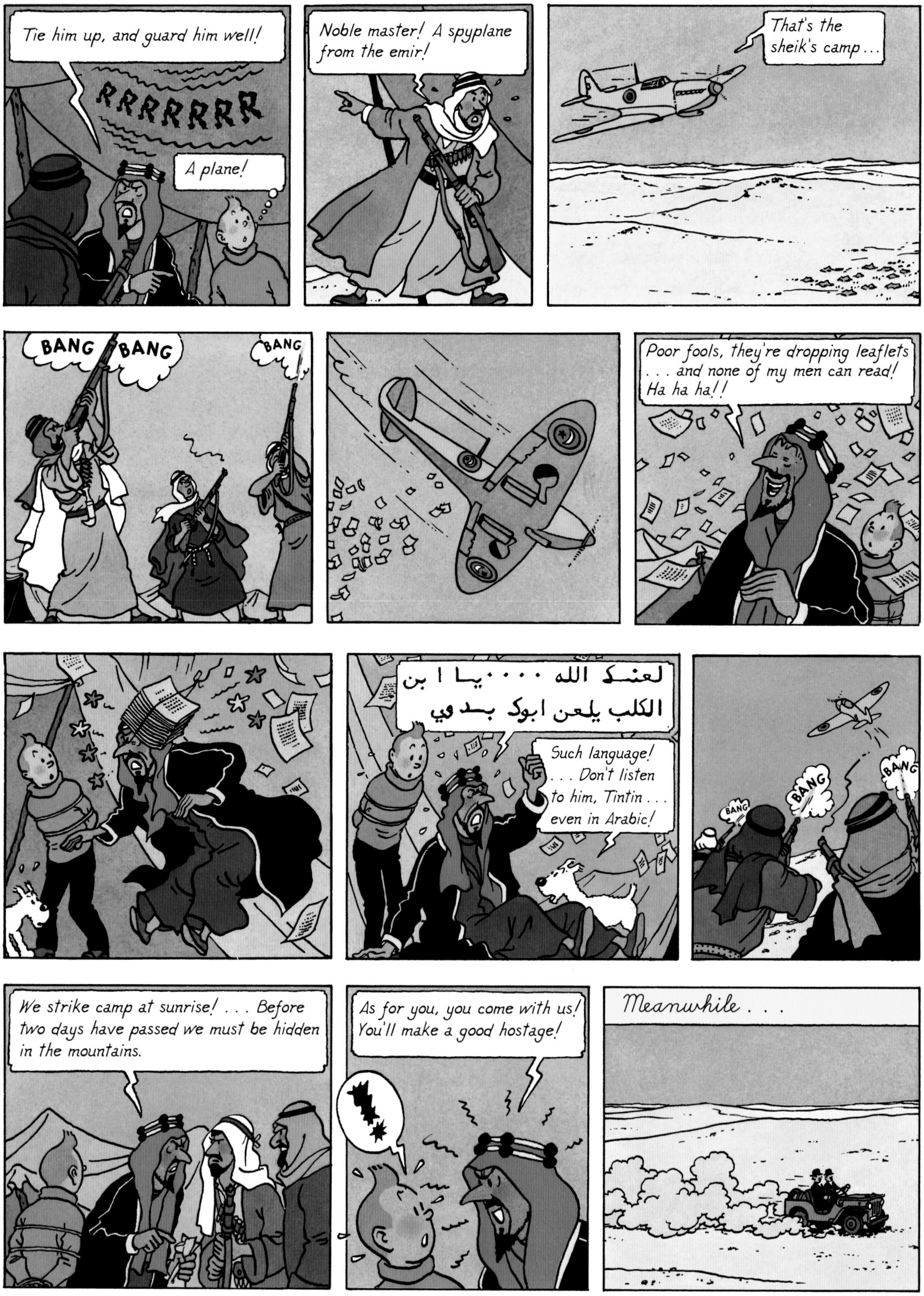
Tie him up, and guard him well!
RRRRRRR
A plane!
Noble master! A spyplane from the emir!
That's the sheik's camp...
BANG
BANG
BANG
Poor fools, they're dropping leaflets . . . and none of my men can read! Ha ha ha!!
لعنك الله .... يا ابن
الكلب يلعن ابوك بدوي
Such language! . . . Don't listen to him, Tintin . . . even in Arabic!
BANG
BANG
BANG
We strike camp at sunrise! . . . Before two days have passed we must be hidden in the mountains.
As for you, you come with us! You'll make a good hostage!
Meanwhile . . .

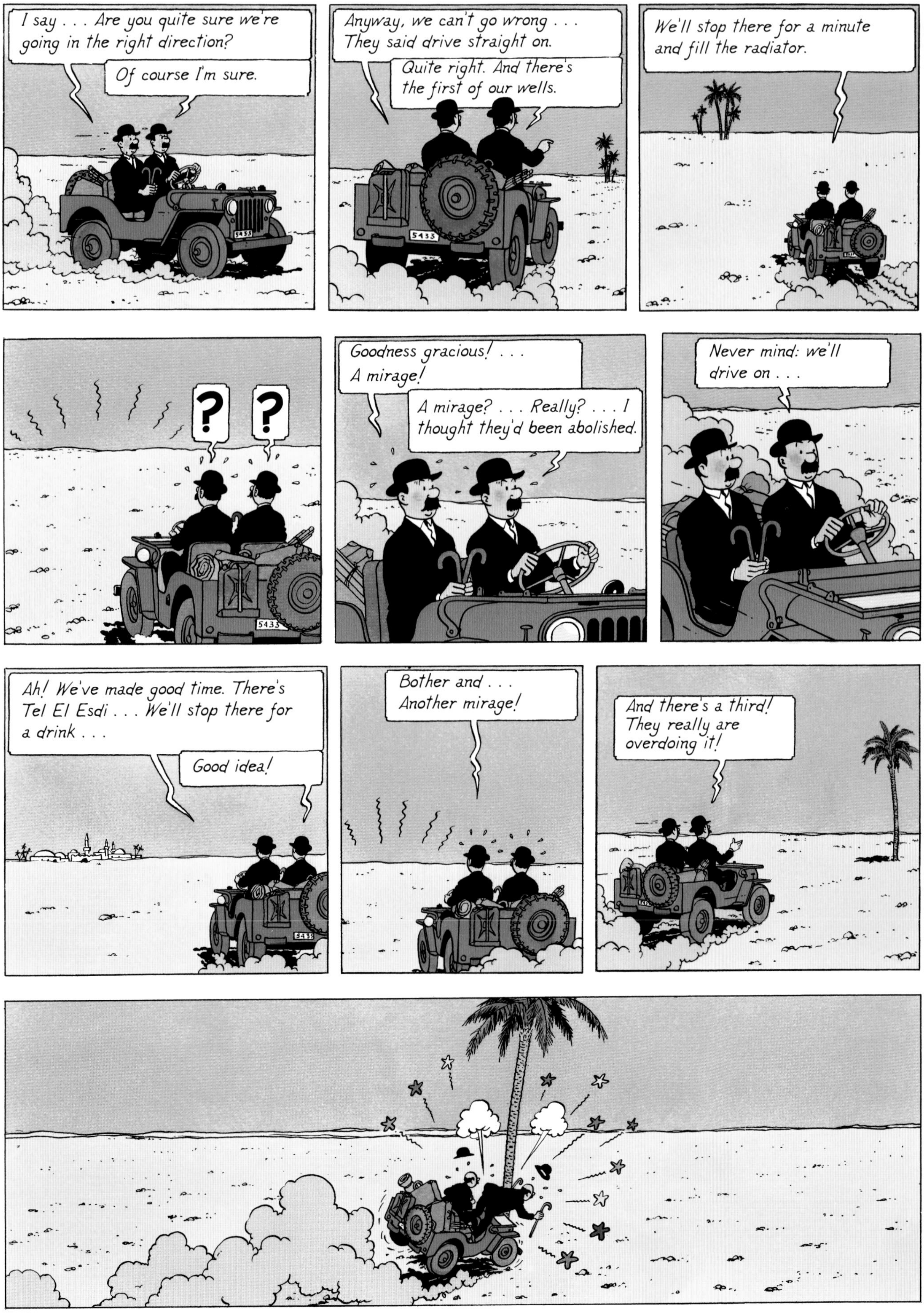

I say . . . Are you quite sure we're going in the right direction?
Of course I'm sure.
Anyway, we can't go wrong . . . They said drive straight on.
Quite right. And there's the first of our wells.
We'll stop there for a minute and fill the radiator.
?
?
Goodness gracious! . . . A mirage!
A mirage? . . . Really? . . . I thought they'd been abolished.
Never mind: we'll drive on . . .
Ah! We've made good time. There's Tel El Esdi . . . We'll stop there for a drink . . .
Good idea!
Bother and . . . Another mirage!
And there's a third! They really are overdoing it!

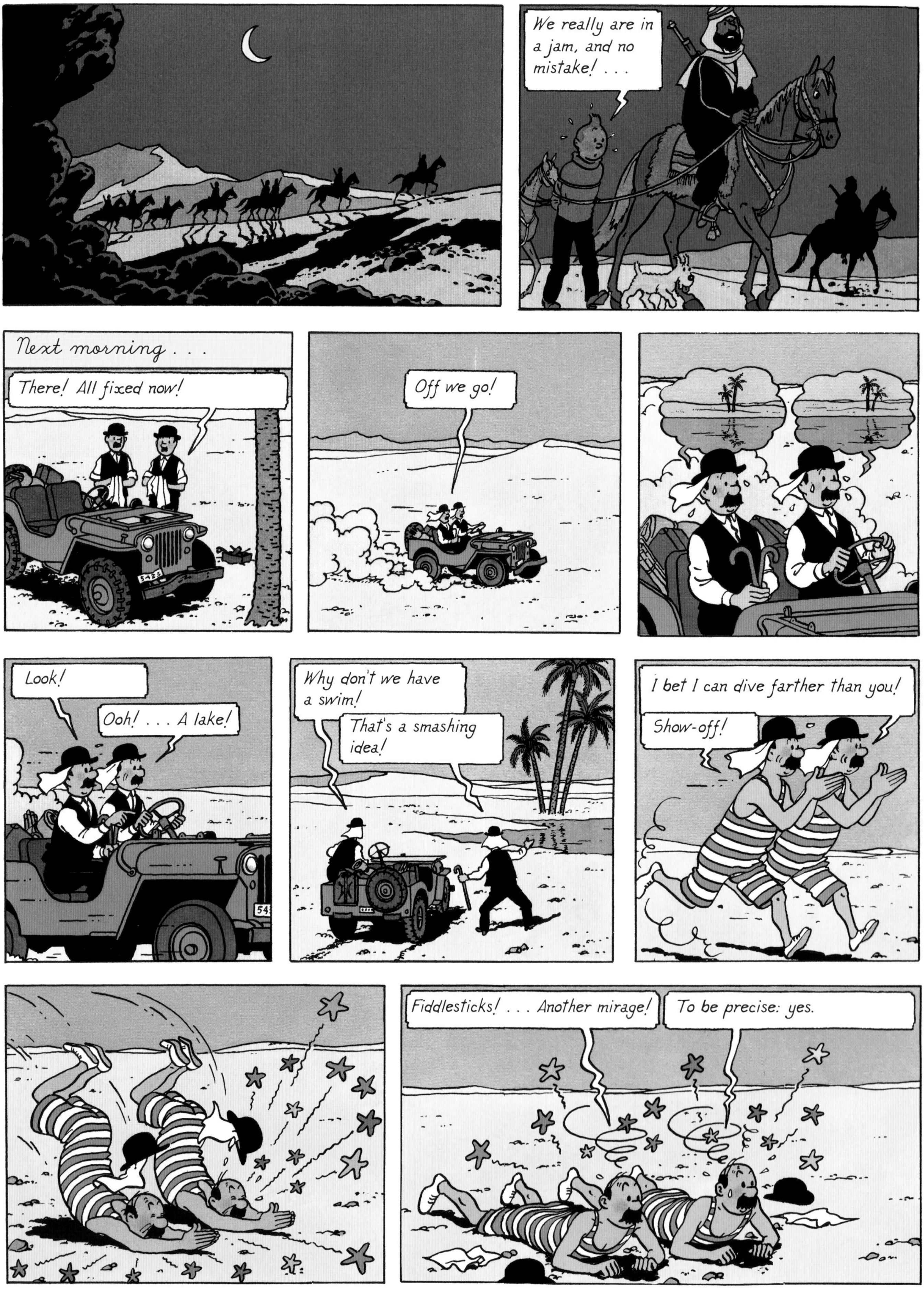
We really are in a jam, and no mistake! . . .
Next morning . . .
There! All fixed now!
Off we go!
Look!
Ooh! . . . A lake!
Why don't we have a swim!
That's a smashing idea!
I bet I can dive farther than you!
Show-off!
Fiddlesticks! . . . Another mirage!
To be precise: yes.

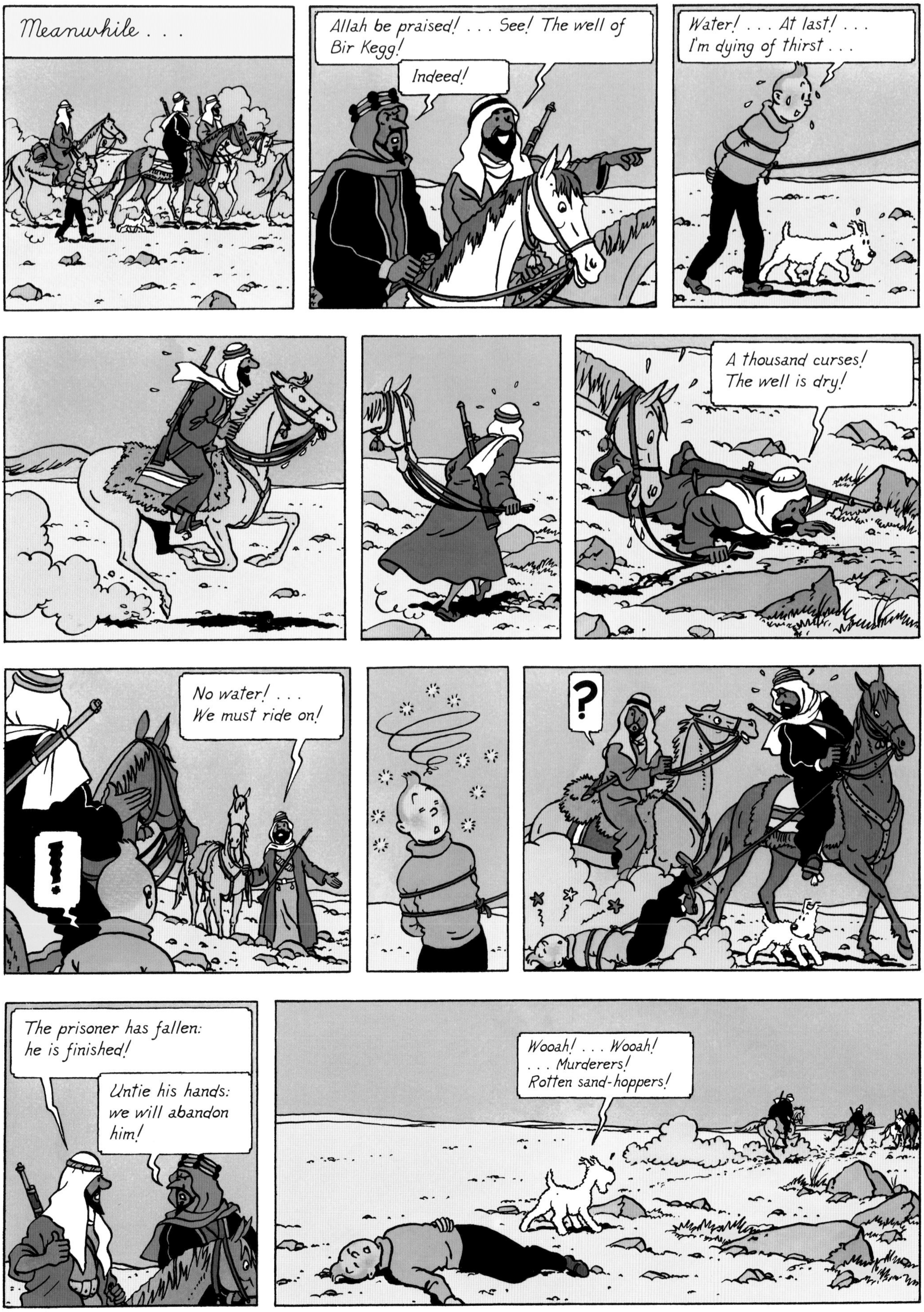
Meanwhile . . .
Allah be praised! . . . See! The well of Bir Kegg!
Indeed!
Water! . . . At last! . . . I'm dying of thirst . . .
A thousand curses! The well is dry!
No water! . . . We must ride on!
?
The prisoner has fallen: he is finished!
Untie his hands: we will abandon him!
Wooah! . . . Wooah! . . . Murderers! Rotten sand-hoppers!

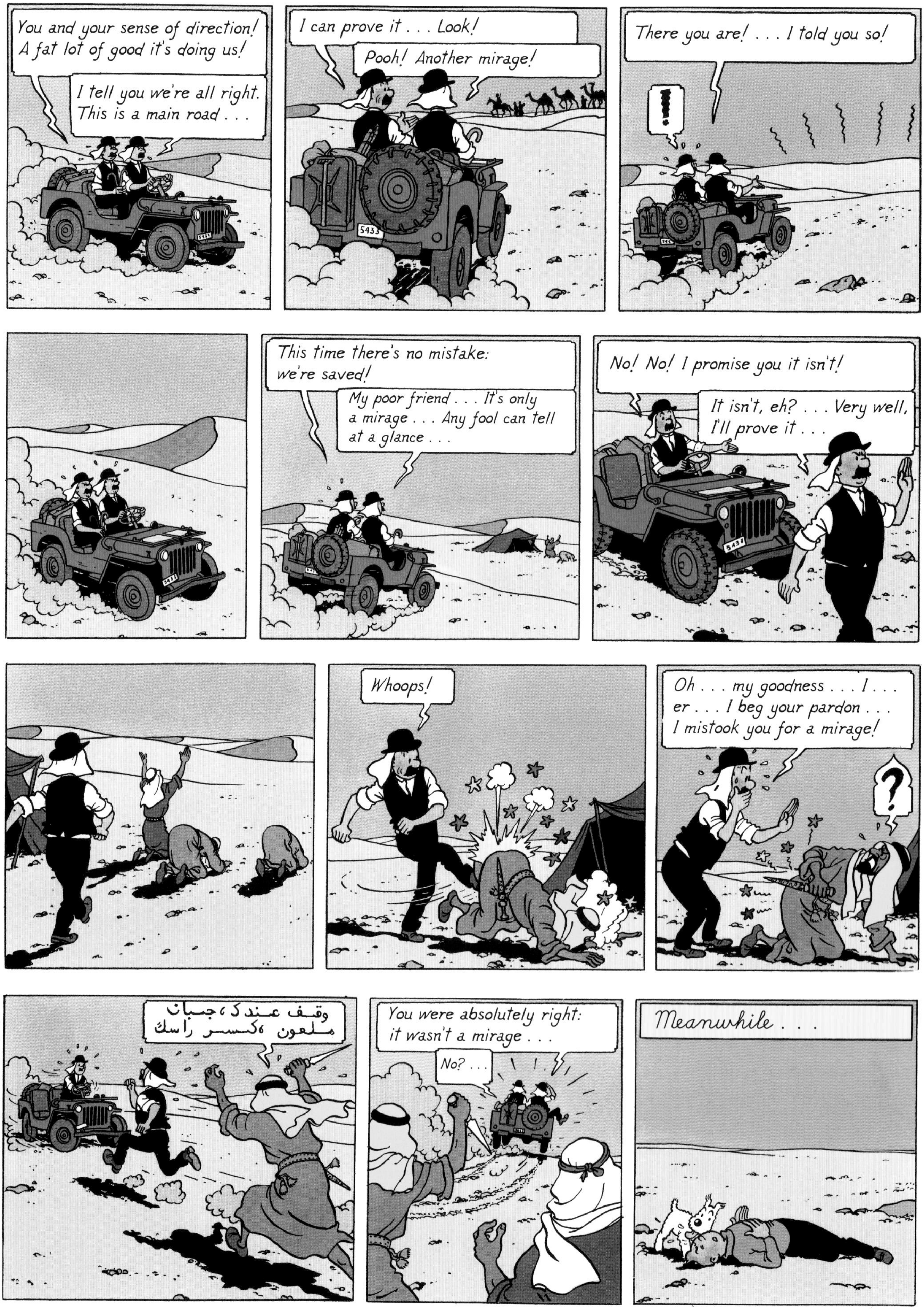
You and your sense of direction! A fat lot of good it's doing us!
I tell you we're all right. This is a main road . . .
I can prove it . . . Look!
Pooh! Another mirage!
There you are! . . . I told you so!
This time there's no mistake: we're saved!
My poor friend . . . It's only a mirage . . . Any fool can tell at a glance . . .
No! No! I promise you it isn't!
It isn't, eh? . . . Very well, I'll prove it . . .
Whoops!
Oh . . . my goodness . . . I . . . er . . . I beg your pardon . . . I mistook you for a mirage!
?
وقف عندك ، جبان
ملعون ،كسر راسك
You were absolutely right: it wasn't a mirage . . .
No? . . .
Meanwhile . . .

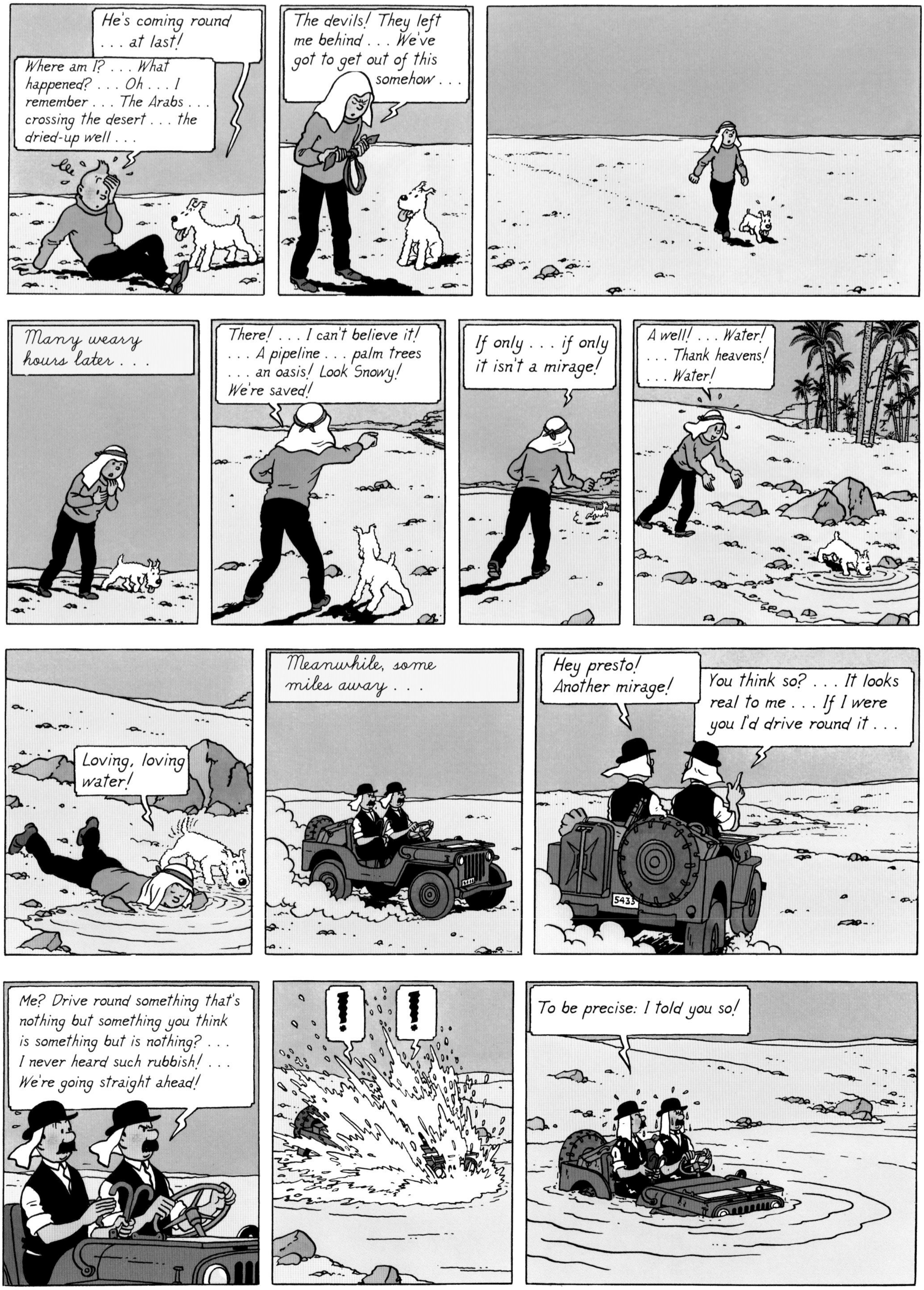
He's coming round . . . at last!
Where am I? . . . What happened? . . . Oh . . . I remember . . . The Arabs . . . crossing the desert . . . the dried-up well . . .
The devils! They left me behind . . . We've got to get out of this somehow . . .
Many weary hours later . . .
There! . . . I can't believe it! . . . A pipeline . . . palm trees . . . an oasis! Look Snowy! We're saved!
If only . . . if only it isn't a mirage!
A well! . . . Water! . . . Thank heavens! . . . Water!
Loving, loving water!
Meanwhile, some miles away . . .
Hey presto! Another mirage!
You think so? . . . It looks real to me . . . If I were you I'd drive round it . . .
5433
Me? Drive round something that's nothing but something you think is something but is nothing? . . . I never heard such rubbish! . . . We're going straight ahead!
!!
!!
To be precise: I told you so!

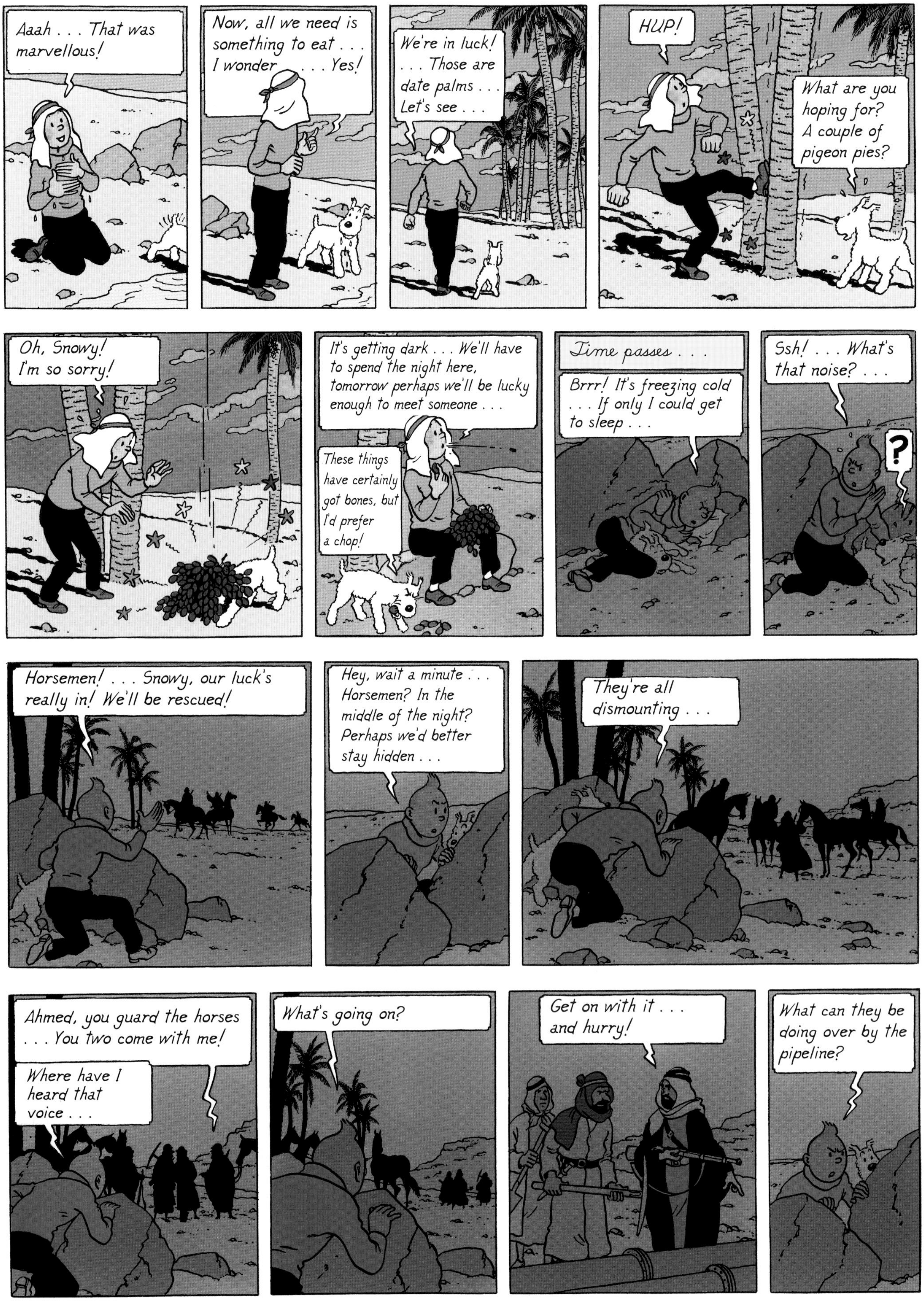
Aaah . . . That was marvellous!
Now, all we need is something to eat . . . I wonder . . . Yes!
We're in luck! . . . Those are date palms . . . Let's see . . .
HUP!
What are you hoping for? A couple of pigeon pies?
Oh, Snowy! I'm so sorry!
It's getting dark . . . We'll have to spend the night here, tomorrow perhaps we'll be lucky enough to meet someone . . .
These things have certainly got bones, but I'd prefer a chop!
Time passes . . .
Brrr! It's freezing cold . . . If only I could get to sleep . . .
Ssh! . . . What's that noise? . . .
?
Horsemen! . . . Snowy, our luck's really in! We'll be rescued!
Hey, wait a minute . . . Horsemen? In the middle of the night? Perhaps we'd better stay hidden . . .
They're all dismounting . . .
Ahmed, you guard the horses . . . You two come with me!
Where have I heard that voice . . .
What's going on?
Get on with it . . . and hurry!
What can they be doing over by the pipeline?

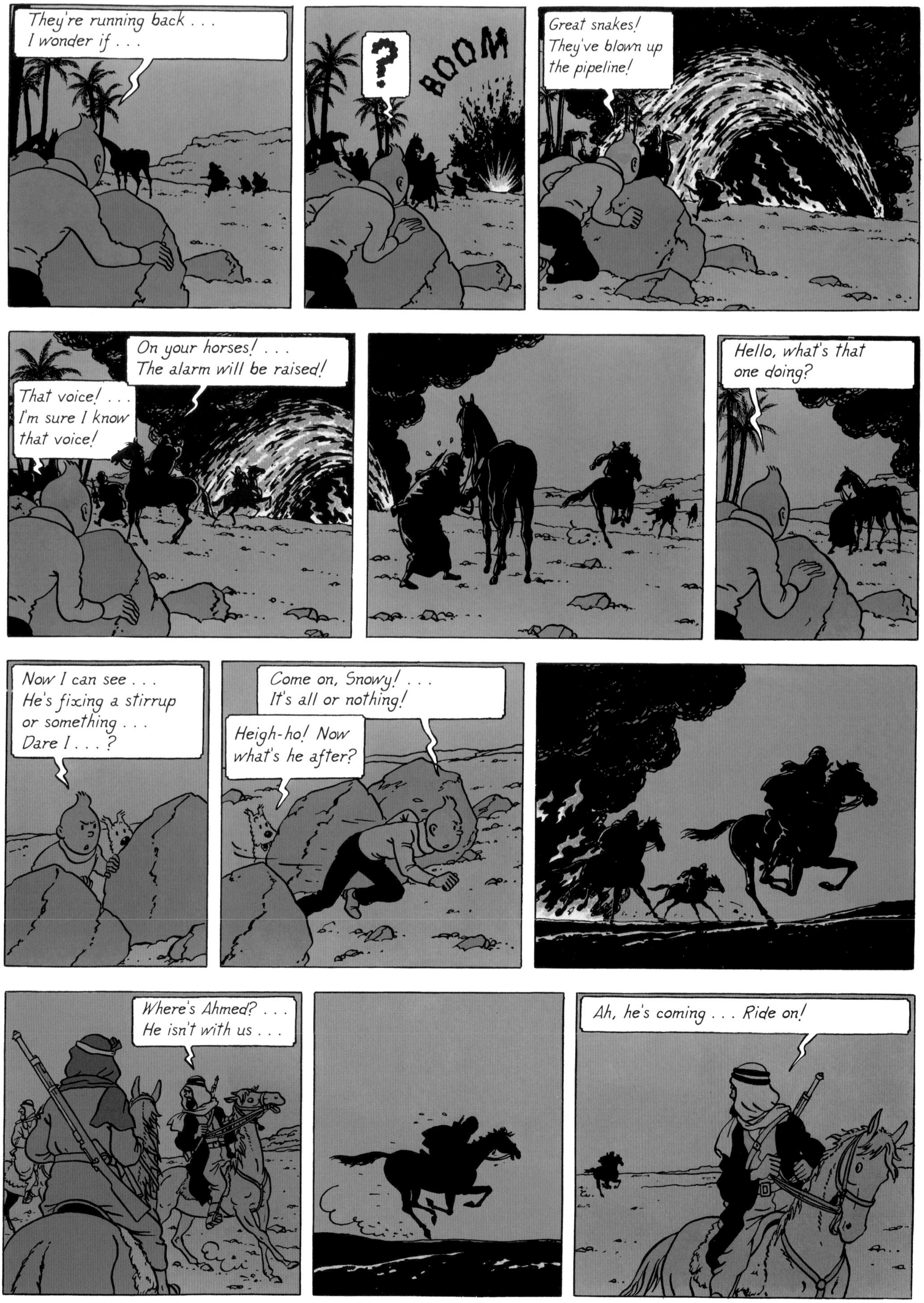
They're running back . . . I wonder if . . .
?
BOOM
Great snakes! They've blown up the pipeline!
On your horses! . . . The alarm will be raised!
That voice! . . . I'm sure I know that voice!
Hello, what's that one doing?
Now I can see . . . He's fixing a stirrup or something . . . Dare I . . . ?
Come on, Snowy! . . . It's all or nothing!
Heigh-ho! Now what's he after?
Where's Ahmed? . . . He isn't with us . . .
Ah, he's coming . . . Ride on!

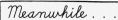

Meanwhile . . .

Hello . . . hello . . . pumping station twelve reporting total loss of pressure . . . pipe must be broken above this station . . . Please send a repair-gang immediately . . .

I must be mad . . . This is crazy . . . But it's too late now. I've taken a chance and can't turn back . . .

Hello . . . Hello . . . Pumping station eleven? . . . Number one control here . . . Close all valves immediately . . . The pipe's fractured between you and number twelve . . . A repair-gang is on the way . . .

This is where we separate . . . It will confuse any pursuers . . . Ahmed will come with me . . .

Where in the world have I heard that voice?

Whoa!

Hold my horse . . . Wait here . . . I'll be back in a moment

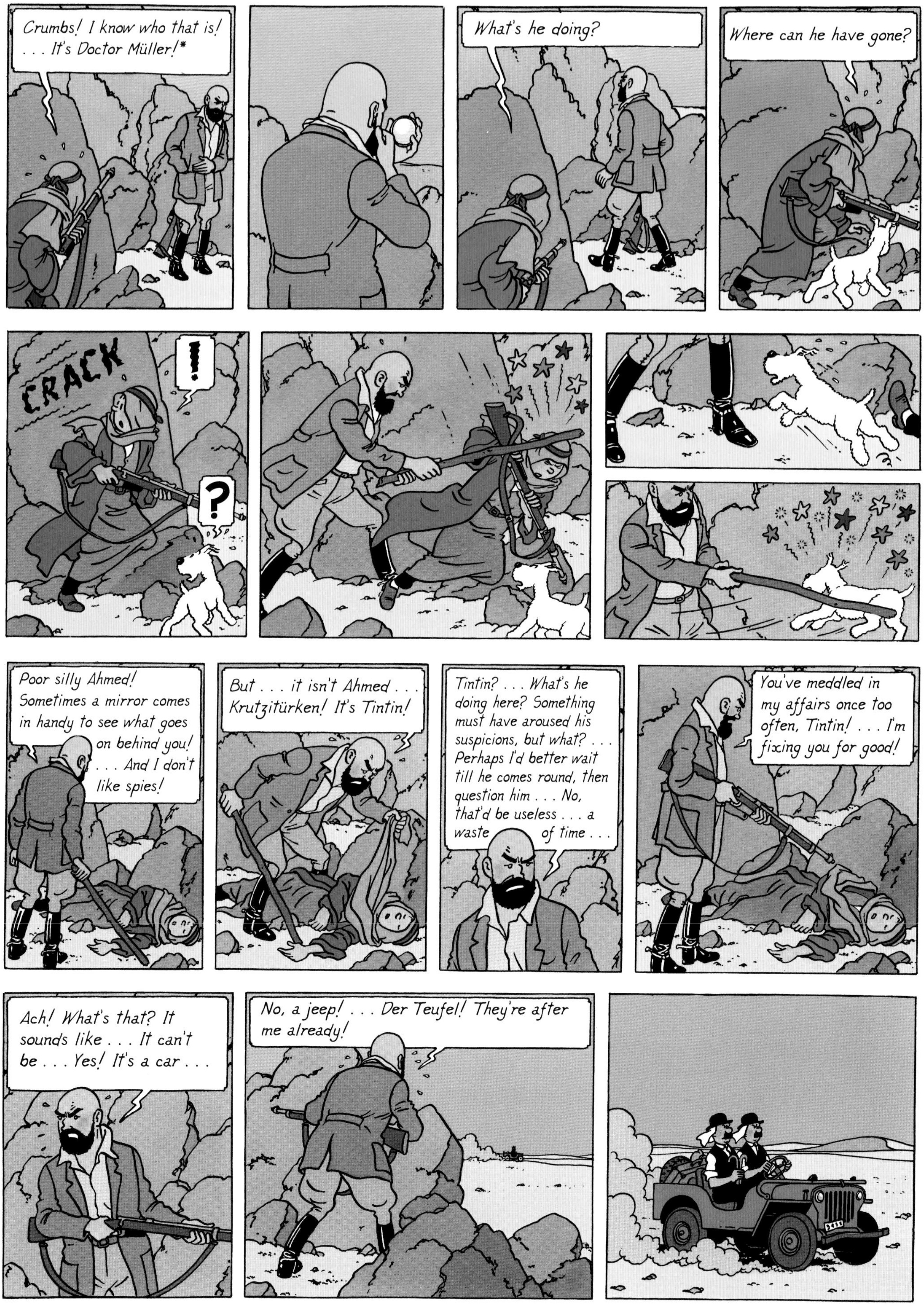
Crumbs! I know who that is! . . . It's Doctor Müller!*
What's he doing?
Where can he have gone?
CRACK
!
?
Poor silly Ahmed! Sometimes a mirror comes in handy to see what goes on behind you! . . . And I don't like spies!
But . . . it isn't Ahmed . . . Krutzitürken! It's Tintin!
Tintin? . . . What's he doing here? Something must have aroused his suspicions, but what? . . . Perhaps I'd better wait till he comes round, then question him . . . No, that'd be useless . . . a waste of time . . .
You've meddled in my affairs once too often, Tintin! . . . I'm fixing you for good!
Ach! What's that? It sounds like . . . It can't be . . . Yes! It's a car . . .
No, a jeep! . . . Der Teufel! They're after me already!

* See The Black Island

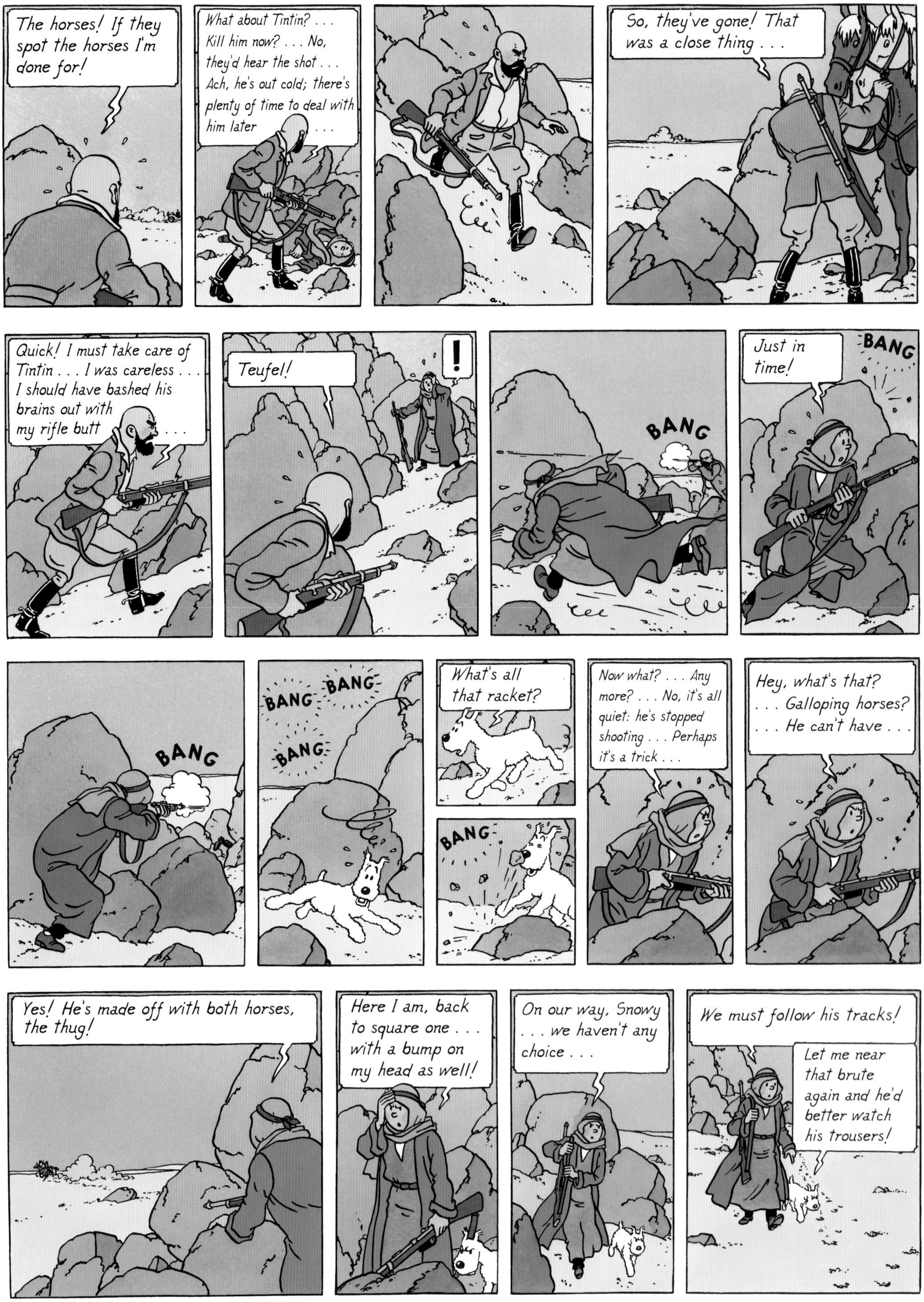

The horses! If they spot the horses I'm done for!
What about Tintin? . . . Kill him now? . . . No, they'd hear the shot . . . Ach, he's out cold; there's plenty of time to deal with him later . . .
So, they've gone! That was a close thing . . .
Quick! I must take care of Tintin . . . I was careless . . . I should have bashed his brains out with my rifle butt . . .
Teufel!
!
BANG
Just in time!
BANG
BANG
BANG
BANG
BANG
What's all that racket?
BANG
Now what? . . . Any more? . . . No, it's all quiet: he's stopped shooting . . . Perhaps it's a trick . . .
Hey, what's that? . . . Galloping horses? . . . He can't have . . .
Yes! He's made off with both horses, the thug!
Here I am, back to square one . . . with a bump on my head as well!
On our way, Snowy . . . we haven't any choice . . .
We must follow his tracks!
Let me near that brute again and he'd better watch his trousers!

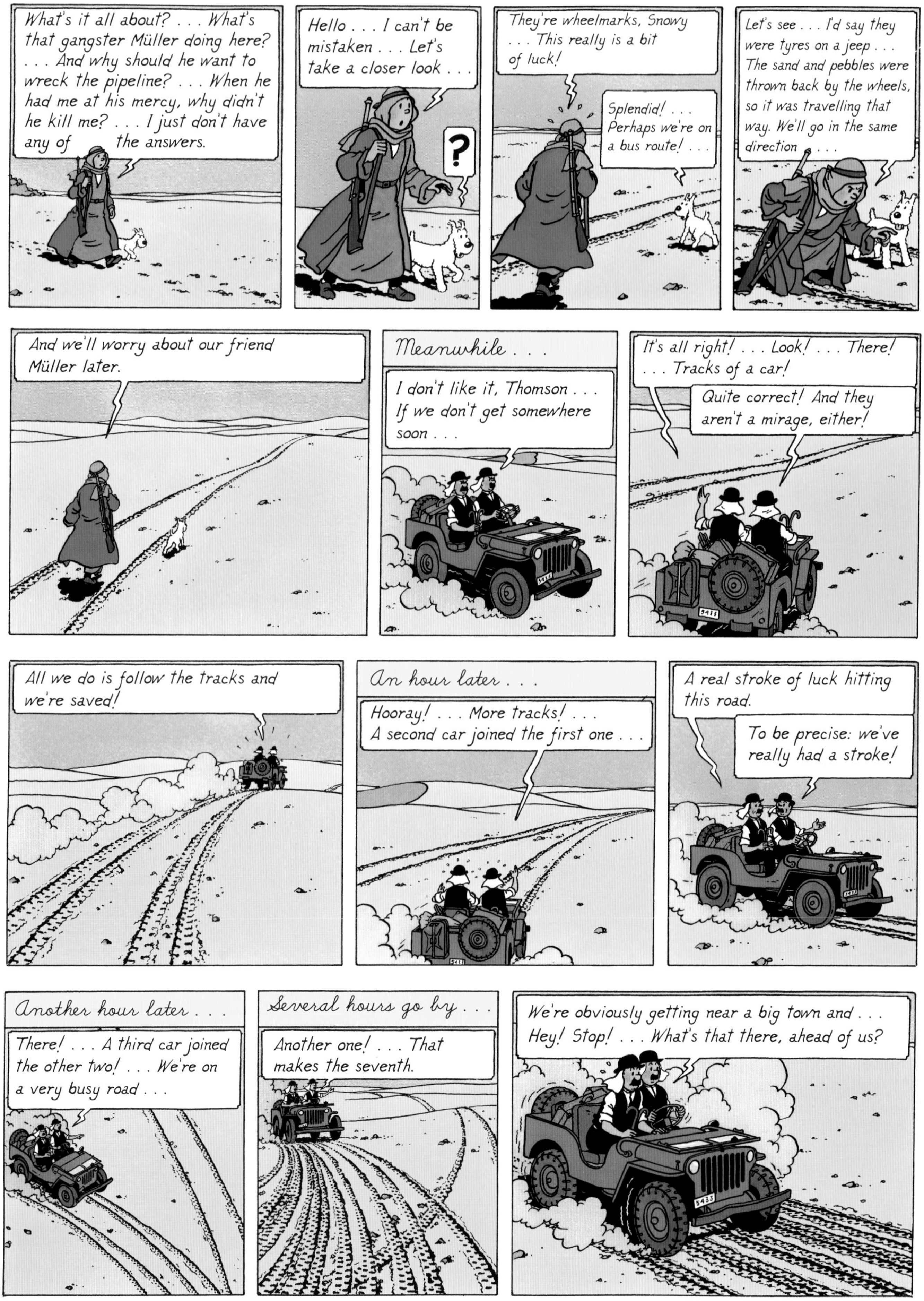
What's it all about? . . . What's that gangster Müller doing here? . . . And why should he want to wreck the pipeline? . . . When he had me at his mercy, why didn't he kill me? . . . I just don't have any of the answers.
Hello . . . I can't be mistaken . . . Let's take a closer look . . .
?
They're wheelmarks, Snowy . . . This really is a bit of luck!
Splendid! . . . Perhaps we're on a bus route! . . .
Let's see . . . I'd say they were tyres on a jeep . . . The sand and pebbles were thrown back by the wheels, so it was travelling that way. We'll go in the same direction . . .
And we'll worry about our friend Müller later.
Meanwhile . . .
I don't like it, Thomson . . . If we don't get somewhere soon . . .
It's all right! . . . Look! . . . There! . . . Tracks of a car!
Quite correct! And they aren't a mirage, either!
All we do is follow the tracks and we're saved!
An hour later . . .
Hooray! . . . More tracks! . . . A second car joined the first one . . .
A real stroke of luck hitting this road.
To be precise: we've really had a stroke!
Another hour later . . .
There! . . . A third car joined the other two! . . . We're on a very busy road . . .
Several hours go by . . .
Another one! . . . That makes the seventh.
We're obviously getting near a big town and . . . Hey! Stop! . . . What's that there, ahead of us?

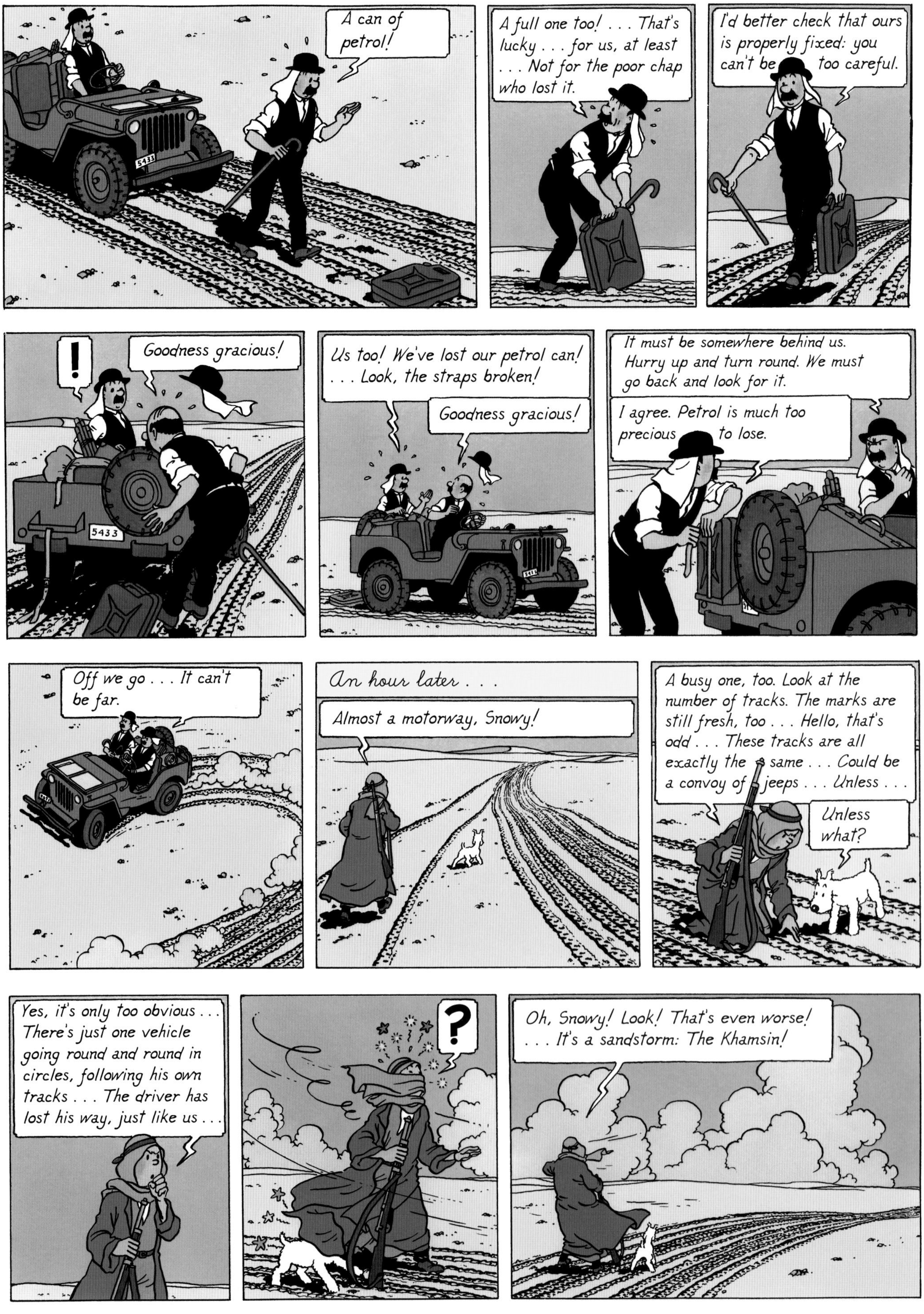
A can of petrol!
A full one too! . . . That's lucky . . . for us, at least . . . Not for the poor chap who lost it.
I'd better check that ours is properly fixed: you can't be too careful.
!
Goodness gracious!
Us too! We've lost our petrol can! . . . Look, the straps broken!
Goodness gracious!
It must be somewhere behind us. Hurry up and turn round. We must go back and look for it.
I agree. Petrol is much too precious to lose.
Off we go . . . It can't be far.
An hour later . . .
Almost a motorway, Snowy!
A busy one, too. Look at the number of tracks. The marks are still fresh, too . . . Hello, that's odd . . . These tracks are all exactly the same . . . Could be a convoy of jeeps . . . Unless . . .
Unless what?
Yes, it's only too obvious . . . There's just one vehicle going round and round in circles, following his own tracks . . . The driver has lost his way, just like us . . .
?
Oh, Snowy! Look! That's even worse! . . . It's a sandstorm: The Khamsin!

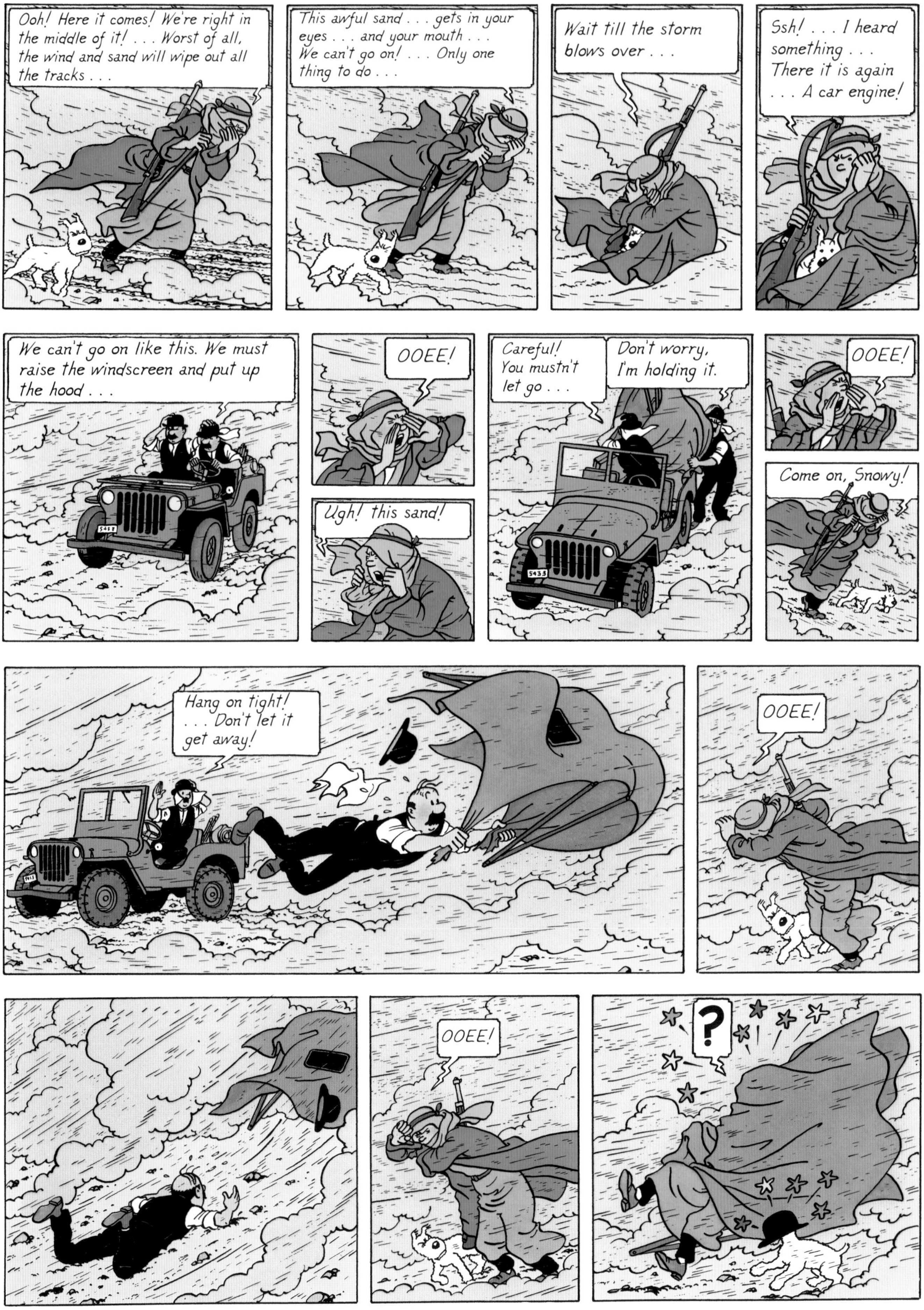
Ooh! Here it comes! We're right in the middle of it! . . . Worst of all, the wind and sand will wipe out all the tracks . . .
This awful sand . . . gets in your eyes . . . and your mouth . . . We can't go on! . . . Only one thing to do . . .
Wait till the storm blows over . . .
Ssh! . . . I heard something . . . There it is again . . . A car engine!
We can't go on like this. We must raise the windscreen and put up the hood . . .
OOEE!
Ugh! this sand!
Careful! You mustn't let go . . .
Don't worry, I'm holding it.
OOEE!
Come on, Snowy!
Hang on tight! . . . Don't let it get away!
OOEE!
OOEE!
?

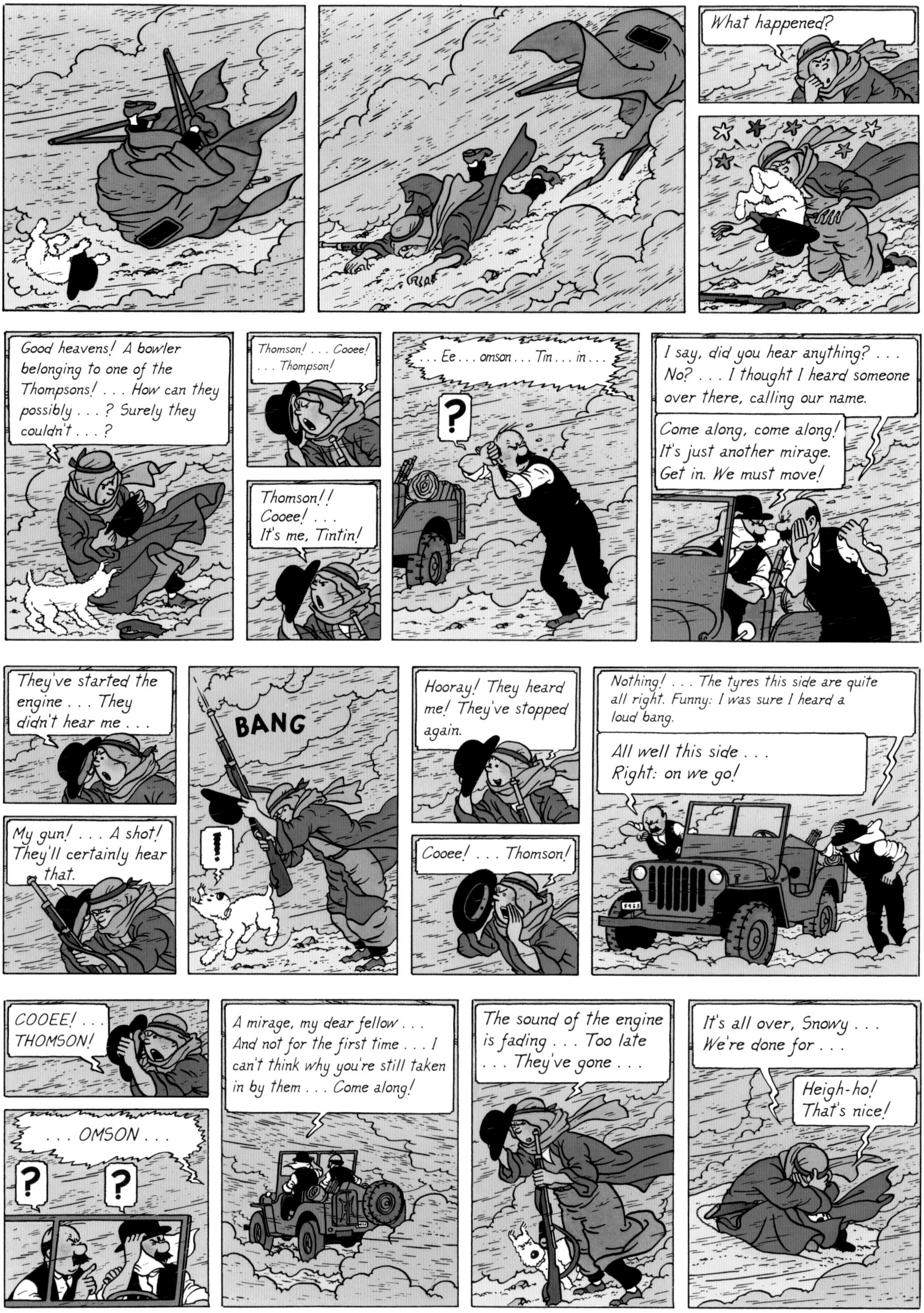
What happened?
Good heavens! A bowler belonging to one of the Thompsons! . . . How can they possibly . . . ? Surely they couldn't . . . ?
Thomson! . . . Cooee! . . . Thompson!
Thomson!! Cooee! . . . It's me, Tintin!
. . . Ee . . . omson . . . Tin . . . in . . .
?
I say, did you hear anything? . . . No? . . . I thought I heard someone over there, calling our name.
Come along, come along! It's just another mirage. Get in. We must move!
They've started the engine . . . They didn't hear me . . .
My gun! . . . A shot! They'll certainly hear that.
BANG
!
Hooray! They heard me! They've stopped again.
Cooee! . . . Thomson!
Nothing! . . . The tyres this side are quite all right. Funny: I was sure I heard a loud bang.
All well this side . . . Right: on we go!
COOEE! . . . THOMSON!
. . . OMSON . . .
?
?
A mirage, my dear fellow . . . And not for the first time . . . I can't think why you're still taken in by them . . . Come along!
The sound of the engine is fading . . . Too late . . . They've gone . . .
It's all over, Snowy . . . We're done for . . .
Heigh-ho! That's nice!

I say . . .   What?

D'you think they talk? . . . Mirages?

Talk? . . . Mirages? . . . What a simple soul you are! Of course they don't talk. Mirages are seen but not heard!

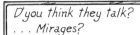

Then what about those shouts we heard just now?

The shouts? . . . I . . . Goodness gracious! You're right: they weren't a mirage! . . . Quick! About turn!

?

The noise of an engine again! They're coming back!

BANG

Look!   Tintin!   It's them!

Found! . . . Found at last! . . . That's marvellous! I'm absolutely overjoyed . . .

My dear old friend Thomson!

. . . to have my hat back! . . . What incredible good fortune!

Later, the storm has died down . . .

Poor Tintin, he was completely worn out. Look: he's fast asleep.

Zzzz Zzzzz

I wish I were too!

Yes, but this isn't the moment!

Zzzz Zzz   Zzzz Zzzz

Zzzzz Zzzzz

Zzzzz Zzzzz

Zzzz Zzzz

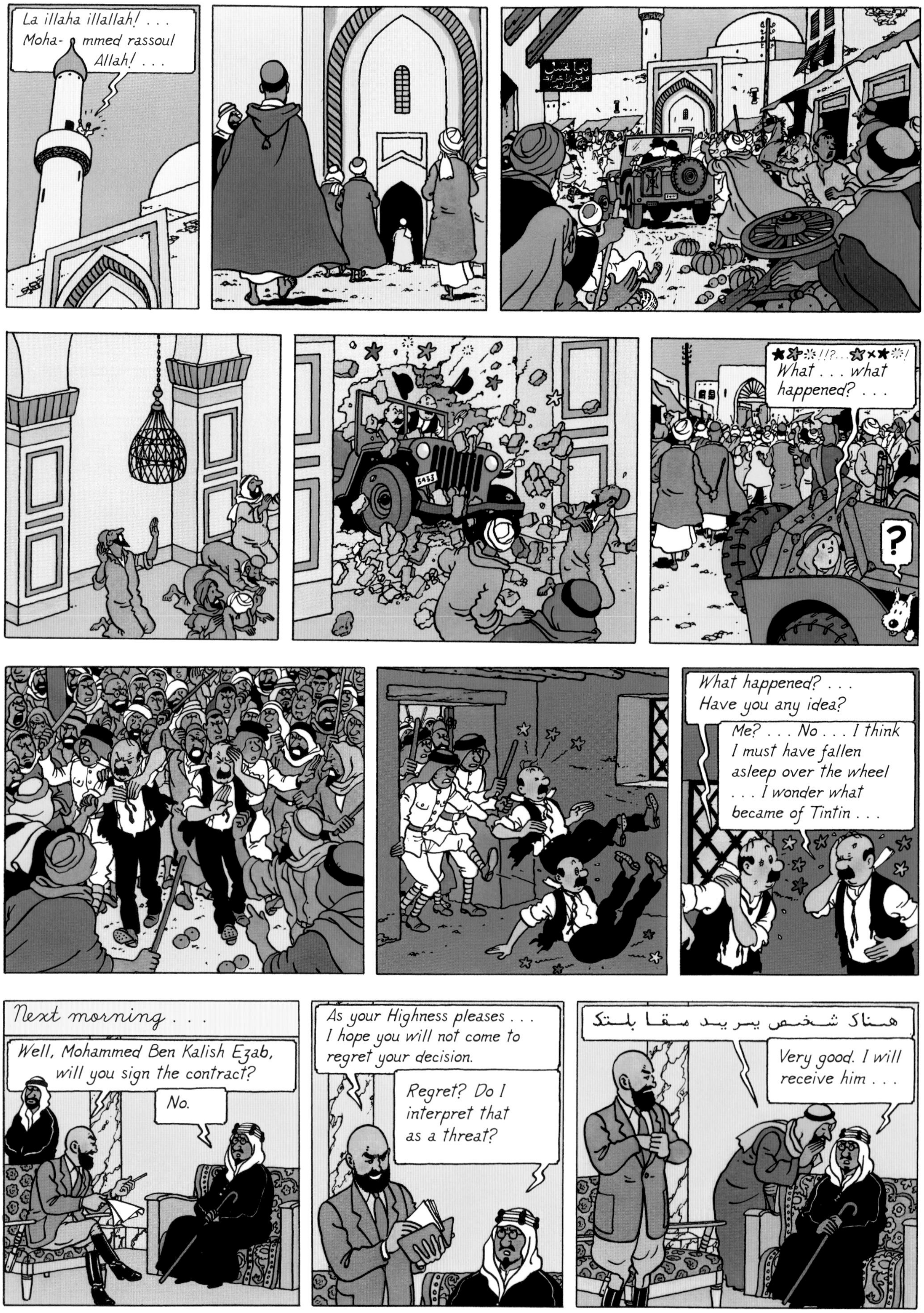
La illaha illallah! . . . Moha- mmed rassoul Allah! . . .
What . . . what happened? . . .
?
What happened? . . . Have you any idea?
Me? . . . No . . . I think I must have fallen asleep over the wheel . . . I wonder what became of Tintin . . .
Next morning . . .
Well, Mohammed Ben Kalish Ezab, will you sign the contract?
No.
As your Highness pleases . . . I hope you will not come to regret your decision.
Regret? Do I interpret that as a threat?
هناك شخص يريد مقابلتك
Very good. I will receive him . . .

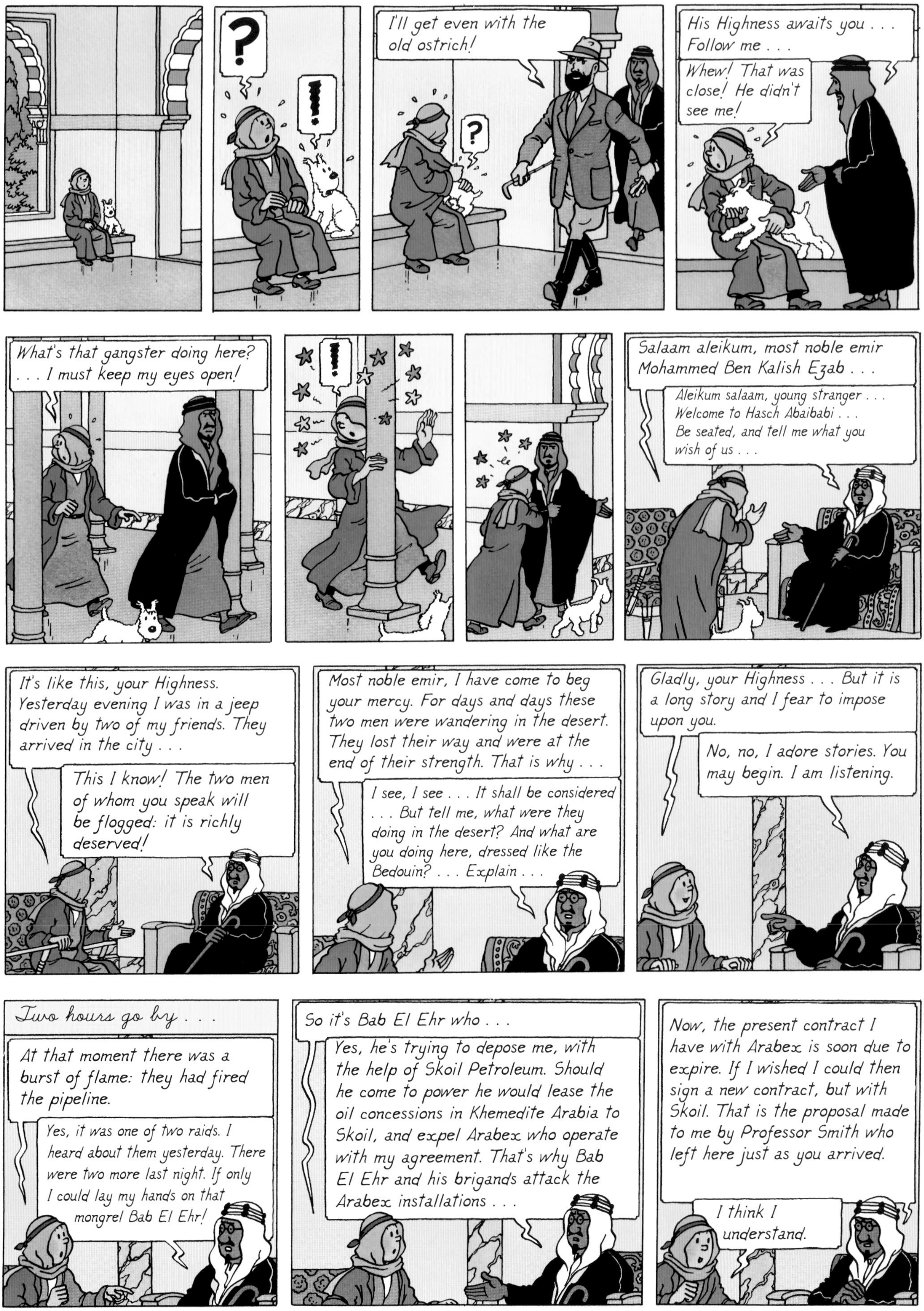
I'll get even with the old ostrich!
His Highness awaits you . . . Follow me . . .
Whew! That was close! He didn't see me!
What's that gangster doing here? . . . I must keep my eyes open!
Salaam aleikum, most noble emir Mohammed Ben Kalish Ezab . . .
Aleikum salaam, young stranger . . . Welcome to Hasch Abaibabi . . . Be seated, and tell me what you wish of us . . .
It's like this, your Highness. Yesterday evening I was in a jeep driven by two of my friends. They arrived in the city . . .
This I know! The two men of whom you speak will be flogged: it is richly deserved!
Most noble emir, I have come to beg your mercy. For days and days these two men were wandering in the desert. They lost their way and were at the end of their strength. That is why . . .
I see, I see . . . It shall be considered . . . But tell me, what were they doing in the desert? And what are you doing here, dressed like the Bedouin? . . . Explain . . .
Gladly, your Highness . . . But it is a long story and I fear to impose upon you.
No, no, I adore stories. You may begin. I am listening.
Two hours go by . . .
At that moment there was a burst of flame: they had fired the pipeline.
Yes, it was one of two raids. I heard about them yesterday. There were two more last night. If only I could lay my hands on that mongrel Bab El Ehr!
So it's Bab El Ehr who . . .
Yes, he's trying to depose me, with the help of Skoil Petroleum. Should he come to power he would lease the oil concessions in Khemedite Arabia to Skoil, and expel Arabex who operate with my agreement. That's why Bab El Ehr and his brigands attack the Arabex installations . . .
Now, the present contract I have with Arabex is soon due to expire. If I wished I could then sign a new contract, but with Skoil. That is the proposal made to me by Professor Smith who left here just as you arrived.
I think I understand.

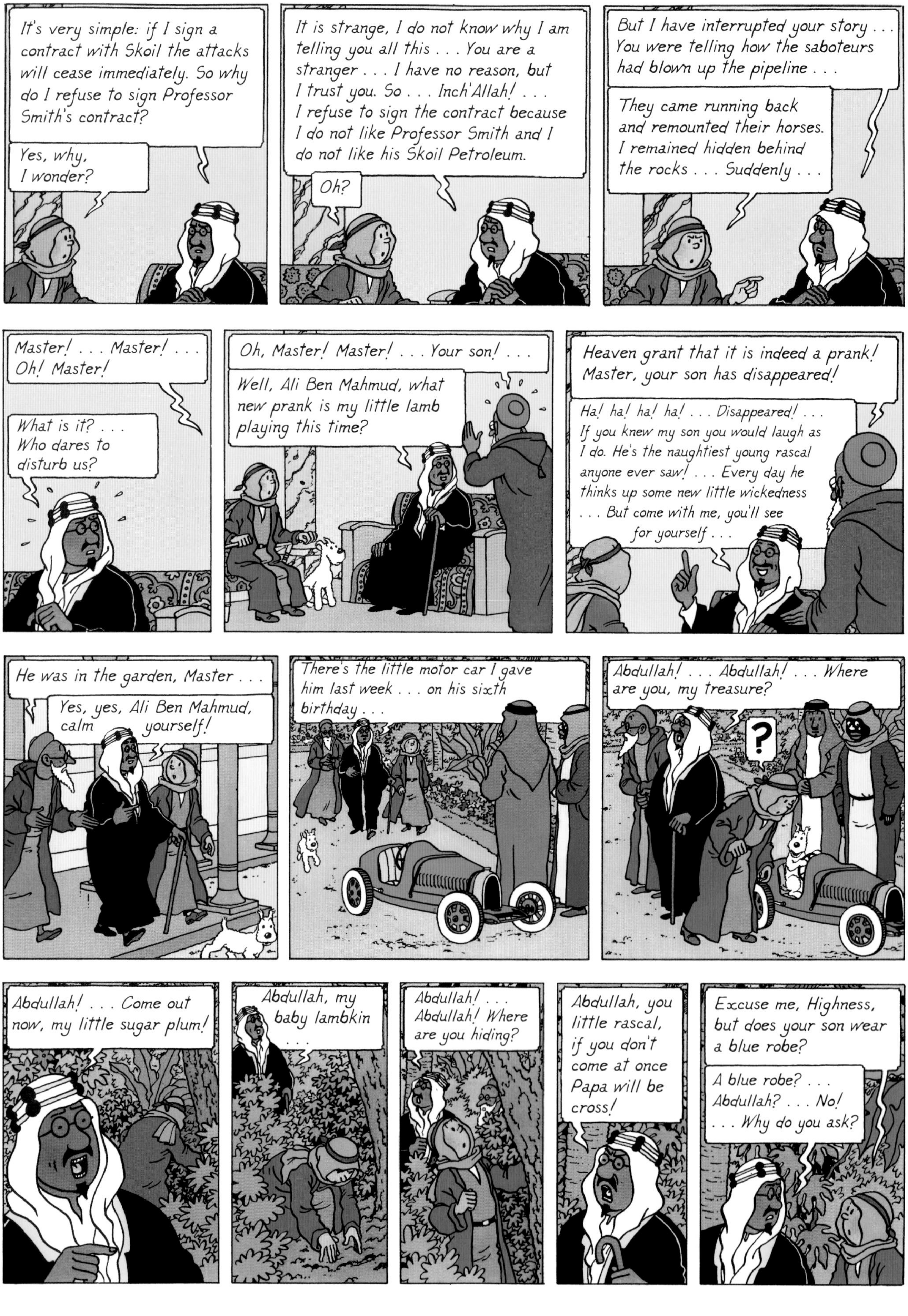

It's very simple: if I sign a contract with Skoil the attacks will cease immediately. So why do I refuse to sign Professor Smith's contract?
Yes, why, I wonder?
It is strange, I do not know why I am telling you all this . . . You are a stranger . . . I have no reason, but I trust you. So . . . Inch'Allah! . . . I refuse to sign the contract because I do not like Professor Smith and I do not like his Skoil Petroleum.
Oh?
But I have interrupted your story . . . You were telling how the saboteurs had blown up the pipeline . . .
They came running back and remounted their horses. I remained hidden behind the rocks . . . Suddenly . . .
Master! . . . Master! . . . Oh! Master!
What is it? . . . Who dares to disturb us?
Oh, Master! Master! . . . Your son! . . .
Well, Ali Ben Mahmud, what new prank is my little lamb playing this time?
Heaven grant that it is indeed a prank! Master, your son has disappeared!
Ha! ha! ha! ha! . . . Disappeared! . . . If you knew my son you would laugh as I do. He's the naughtiest young rascal anyone ever saw! . . . Every day he thinks up some new little wickedness . . . But come with me, you'll see for yourself . . .
He was in the garden, Master . . .
Yes, yes, Ali Ben Mahmud, calm yourself!
There's the little motor car I gave him last week . . . on his sixth birthday . . .
Abdullah! . . . Abdullah! . . . Where are you, my treasure?
?
Abdullah! . . . Come out now, my little sugar plum!
Abdullah, my baby lambkin . . .
Abdullah! . . . Abdullah! Where are you hiding?
Abdullah, you little rascal, if you don't come at once Papa will be cross!
Excuse me, Highness, but does your son wear a blue robe?
A blue robe? . . . Abdullah? . . . No! . . . Why do you ask?

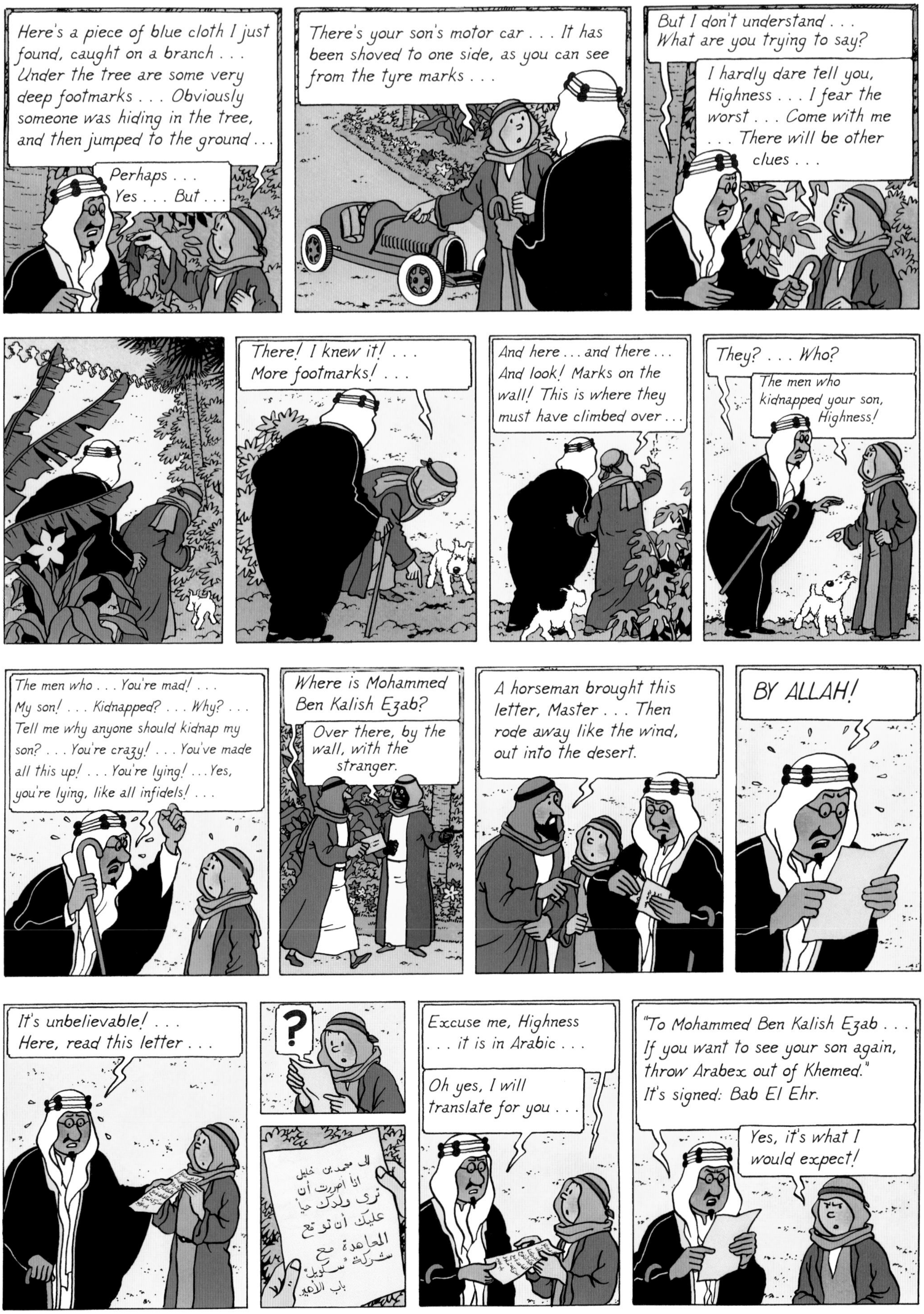

Here's a piece of blue cloth I just found, caught on a branch . . . Under the tree are some very deep footmarks . . . Obviously someone was hiding in the tree, and then jumped to the ground . . .
Perhaps . . . Yes . . . But . . .
There's your son's motor car . . . It has been shoved to one side, as you can see from the tyre marks . . .
But I don't understand . . . What are you trying to say?
I hardly dare tell you, Highness . . . I fear the worst . . . Come with me . . . There will be other clues . . .
There! I knew it! . . . More footmarks! . . .
And here . . . and there . . . And look! Marks on the wall! This is where they must have climbed over . . .
They? . . . Who?
The men who kidnapped your son, Highness!
The men who . . . You're mad! . . . My son! . . . Kidnapped? . . . Why? . . . Tell me why anyone should kidnap my son? . . . You're crazy! . . . You've made all this up! . . . You're lying! . . . Yes, you're lying, like all infidels! . . .
Where is Mohammed Ben Kalish Ezab?
Over there, by the wall, with the stranger.
A horseman brought this letter, Master . . . Then rode away like the wind, out into the desert.
BY ALLAH!
It's unbelievable! . . . Here, read this letter . . .
?
Excuse me, Highness . . . it is in Arabic . . .
Oh yes, I will translate for you . . .
"To Mohammed Ben Kalish Ezab . . . If you want to see your son again, throw Arabex out of Khemed." It's signed: Bab El Ehr.
Yes, it's what I would expect!

Bab El Ehr! Bab El Ehr! Son of a mangy dog! . . . Grandson of a scurvy jackal! . . . Great grandson of a moulting vulture! . . . My revenge will be terrible! . . . I will impale you on a spit! . . . I will roast you over a slow fire! . . . I will pull out your beard, one hair at a time . . . And I will stuff it down your throat . . .
But we must act! Where is my military adviser?
!
Ohhh! . . . His little car!
Boo-hoo-hoo-ooo-ooo-ooo! . . . My little Abdullah! . . . My little honeybun, where are you? . . . My little peppermint cream . . . Boo-hoo-hoo . . . hoo . . . hoo . . .
Highness, you must calm yourself.
Woo-hoo-hoo . . . My little angel . . . Boo-woo-hoo-hoo!
My little Abdullah! . . . Aaaah . . . Aaaah . . . Aaaah . . . Aaaah . . .
?
TCHOOO! . . . Aaaah . . . TCHOO! . . . Aaaah TCHOOO!
You see . . . Aaaah . . . TCHOOO! . . . It was one of his last tricks: he'd just found out about . . . Aaaah TCHOOO! . . . about Aaaah TCHOOO! . . . about sneezing pow-ow-ow-der! . . . He wanted a box for his birthday . . .
A few minutes later . . .
This is Yussuf Ben Mulfrid, my military adviser. He'll explain his plan of campaign . . . A cigarette?
No, thank you. I don't smoke.
Well, noble master . . . In two hours, three hundred horsemen will be ready to leave in pursuit of Bab El Ehr's followers. I have already given orders for scouts to follow their trail . . . Briefly, I can say to you . . .
PCHTT
Allah is good! . . . My little poppet replaced all my best havanas with his trick cigars . . . Wasn't that sweet? . . .
My one and only little chickadee! . . .
PCHTT
!!!
By the beard of the prophet! That wretched little centipede has changed all my best Sobranies for his filthy joke cigarettes! . . .

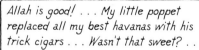

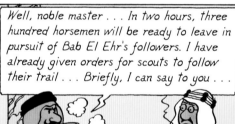

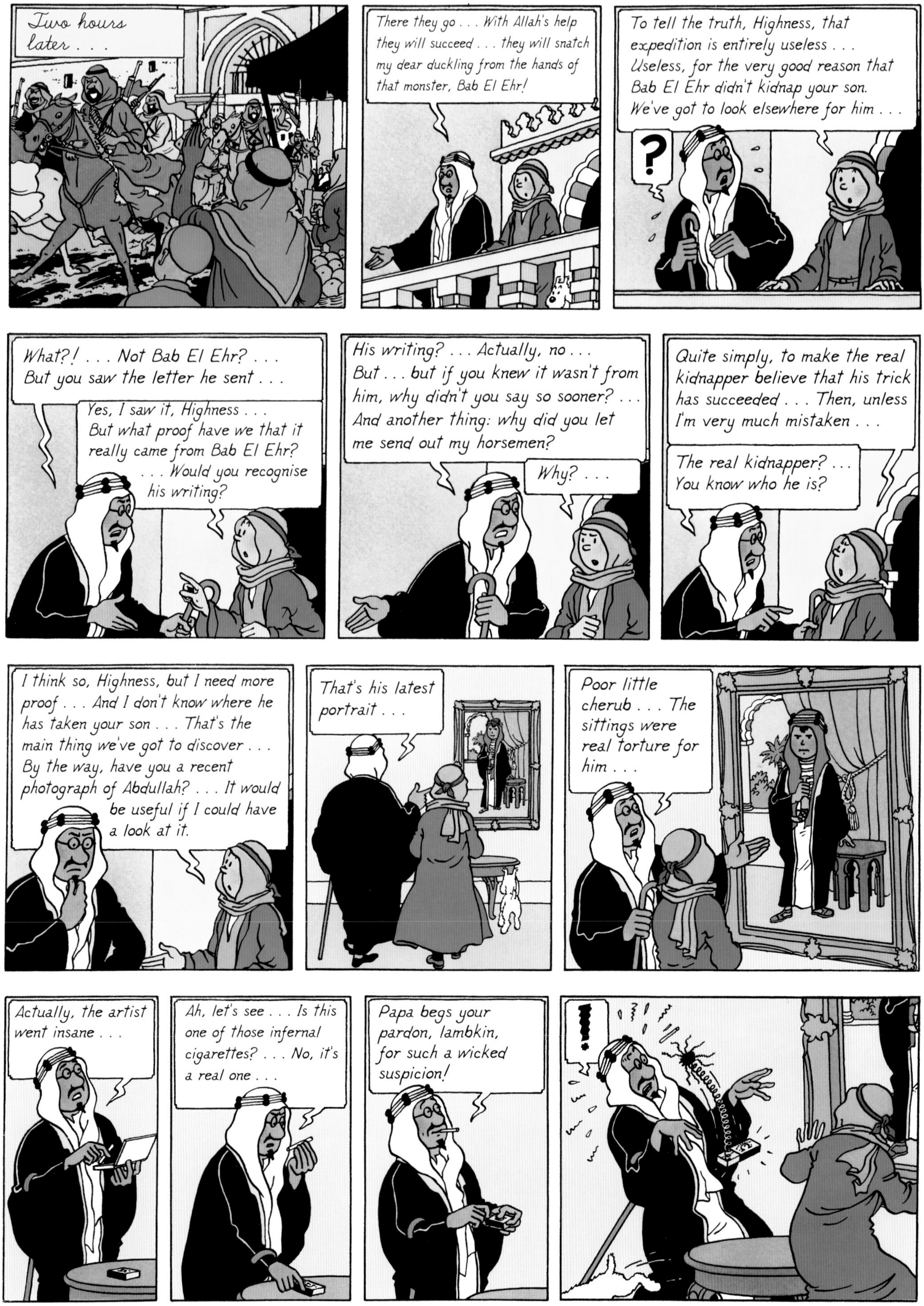
Two hours later . . .
There they go . . . With Allah's help they will succeed . . . they will snatch my dear duckling from the hands of that monster, Bab El Ehr!
To tell the truth, Highness, that expedition is entirely useless . . . Useless, for the very good reason that Bab El Ehr didn't kidnap your son. We've got to look elsewhere for him . . .
?
What?! . . . Not Bab El Ehr? . . . But you saw the letter he sent . . .
Yes, I saw it, Highness . . . But what proof have we that it really came from Bab El Ehr? . . . Would you recognise his writing?
His writing? . . . Actually, no . . . But . . . but if you knew it wasn't from him, why didn't you say so sooner? . . . And another thing: why did you let me send out my horsemen?
Why? . . .
Quite simply, to make the real kidnapper believe that his trick has succeeded . . . Then, unless I'm very much mistaken . . .
The real kidnapper? . . . You know who he is?
I think so, Highness, but I need more proof . . . And I don't know where he has taken your son . . . That's the main thing we've got to discover . . . By the way, have you a recent photograph of Abdullah? . . . It would be useful if I could have a look at it.
That's his latest portrait . . .
Poor little cherub . . . The sittings were real torture for him . . .
Actually, the artist went insane . . .
Ah, let's see . . . Is this one of those infernal cigarettes? . . . No, it's a real one . . .
Papa begs your pardon, lambkin, for such a wicked suspicion!
!!!

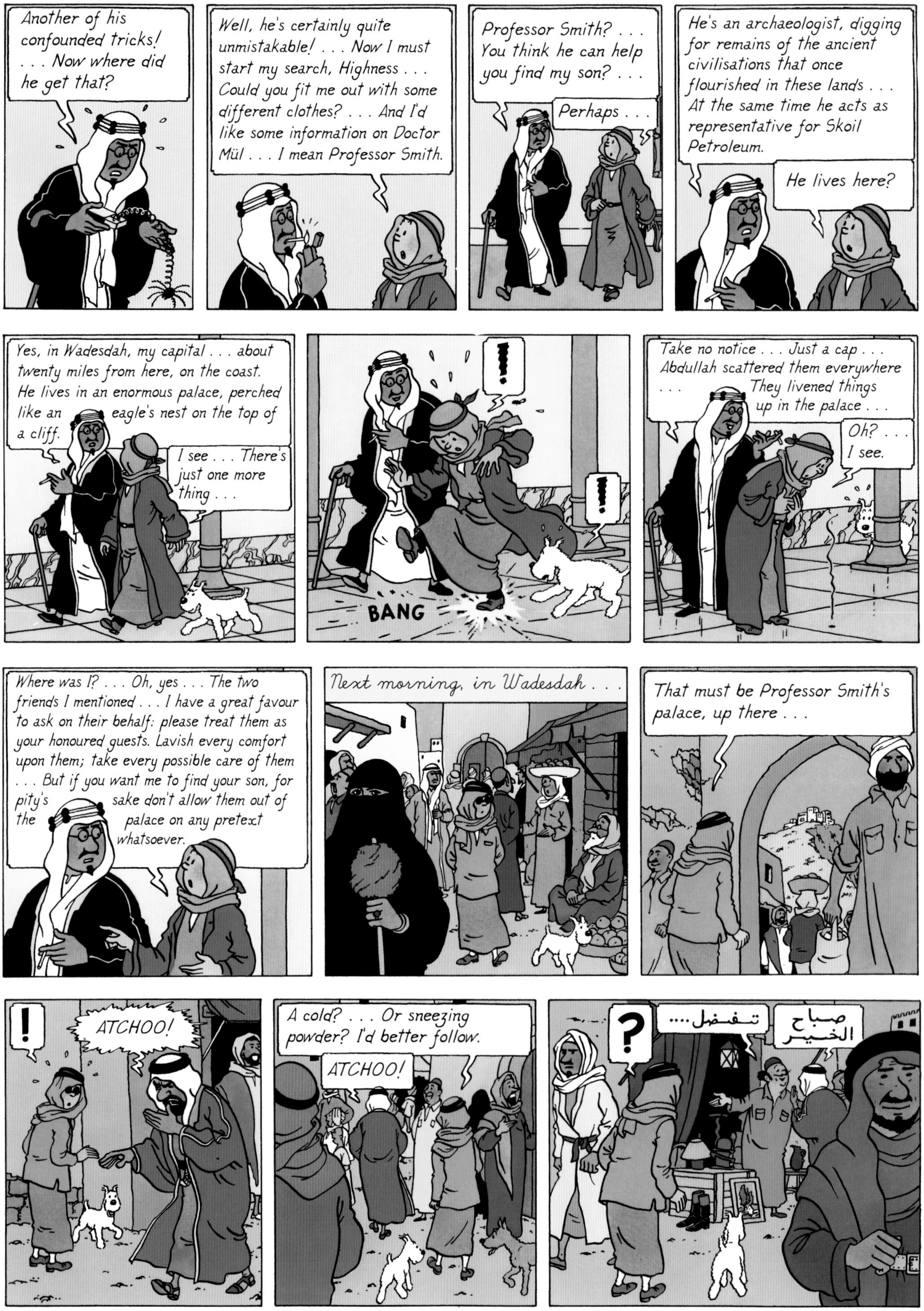

Another of his confounded tricks! . . . Now where did he get that?
Well, he's certainly quite unmistakable! . . . Now I must start my search, Highness . . . Could you fit me out with some different clothes? . . . And I'd like some information on Doctor Mül . . . I mean Professor Smith.
Professor Smith? . . . You think he can help you find my son? . . .
Perhaps . . .
He's an archaeologist, digging for remains of the ancient civilisations that once flourished in these lands . . . At the same time he acts as representative for Skoil Petroleum.
He lives here?
Yes, in Wadesdah, my capital . . . about twenty miles from here, on the coast. He lives in an enormous palace, perched like an eagle's nest on the top of a cliff.
I see . . . There's just one more thing . . .
BANG
Take no notice . . . Just a cap . . . Abdullah scattered them everywhere . . . They livened things up in the palace . . .
Oh? . . . I see.
Where was I? . . . Oh, yes . . . The two friends I mentioned . . . I have a great favour to ask on their behalf: please treat them as your honoured guests. Lavish every comfort upon them; take every possible care of them . . . But if you want me to find your son, for pity's sake don't allow them out of the palace on any pretext whatsoever.
Next morning, in Wadesdah . . .
That must be Professor Smith's palace, up there . . .
!
ATCHOO!
A cold? . . . Or sneezing powder? I'd better follow.
ATCHOO!
?
تفضل....
صباح الخير

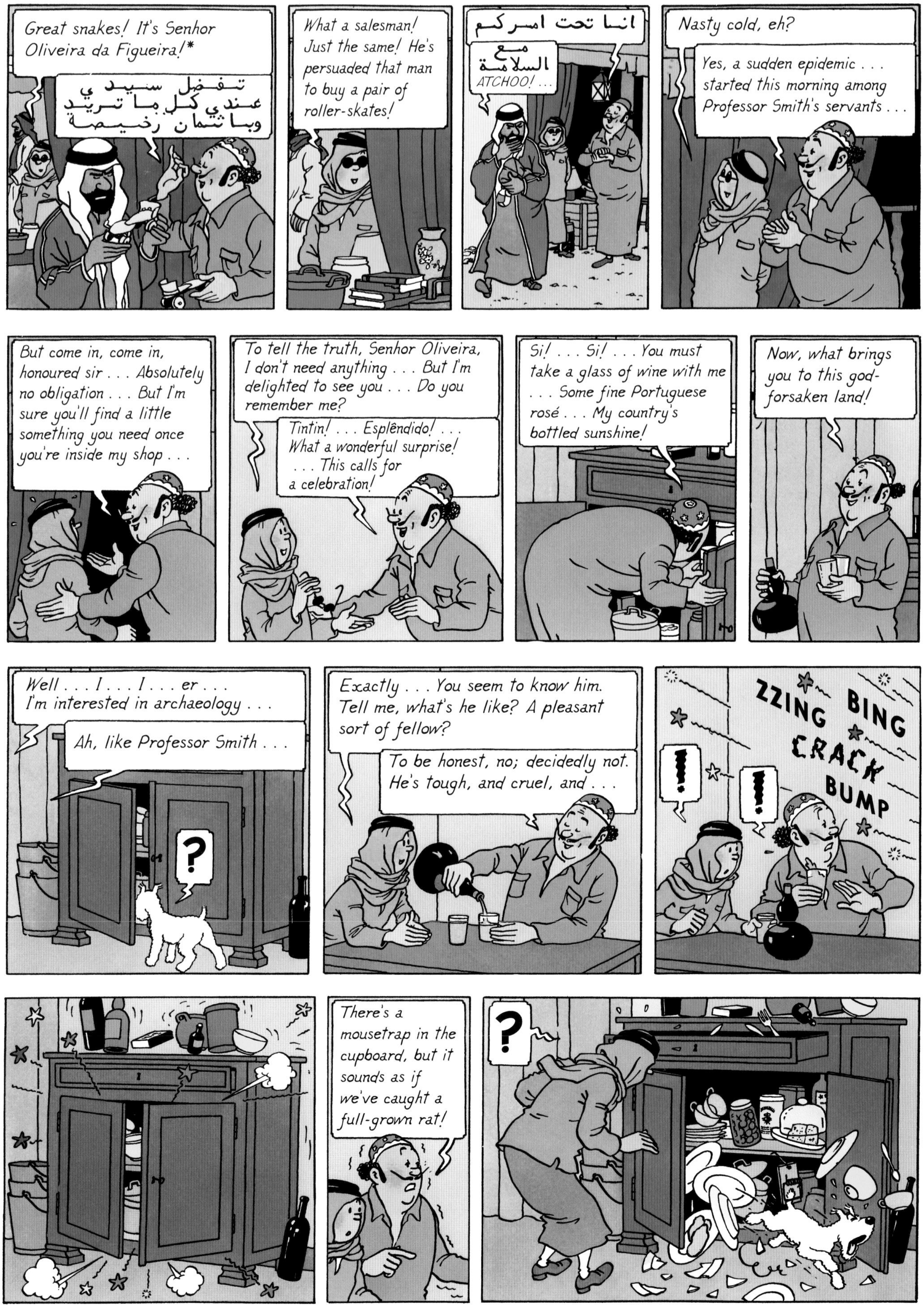
Great snakes! It's Senhor Oliveira da Figueira!*
تفضل سيدي
عندي كل ما تريد
وبا ثمان رخيصة
What a salesman! Just the same! He's persuaded that man to buy a pair of roller-skates!
انا تحت امركم
مع السلامة
ATCHOO! . . .
Nasty cold, eh?
Yes, a sudden epidemic . . . started this morning among Professor Smith's servants . . .
But come in, come in, honoured sir . . . Absolutely no obligation . . . But I'm sure you'll find a little something you need once you're inside my shop . . .
To tell the truth, Senhor Oliveira, I don't need anything . . . But I'm delighted to see you . . . Do you remember me?
Tintin! . . . Esplêndido! . . . What a wonderful surprise! . . . This calls for a celebration!
Si! . . . Si! . . . You must take a glass of wine with me . . . Some fine Portuguese rosé . . . My country's bottled sunshine!
Now, what brings you to this god-forsaken land!
Well . . . I . . . I . . . er . . . I'm interested in archaeology . . .
Ah, like Professor Smith . . .
?
Exactly . . . You seem to know him. Tell me, what's he like? A pleasant sort of fellow?
To be honest, no; decidedly not. He's tough, and cruel, and . . .
ZZING
BING
CRACK
BUMP
!
!
There's a mousetrap in the cupboard, but it sounds as if we've caught a full-grown rat!
?

* See Cigars of the Pharaoh

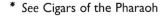

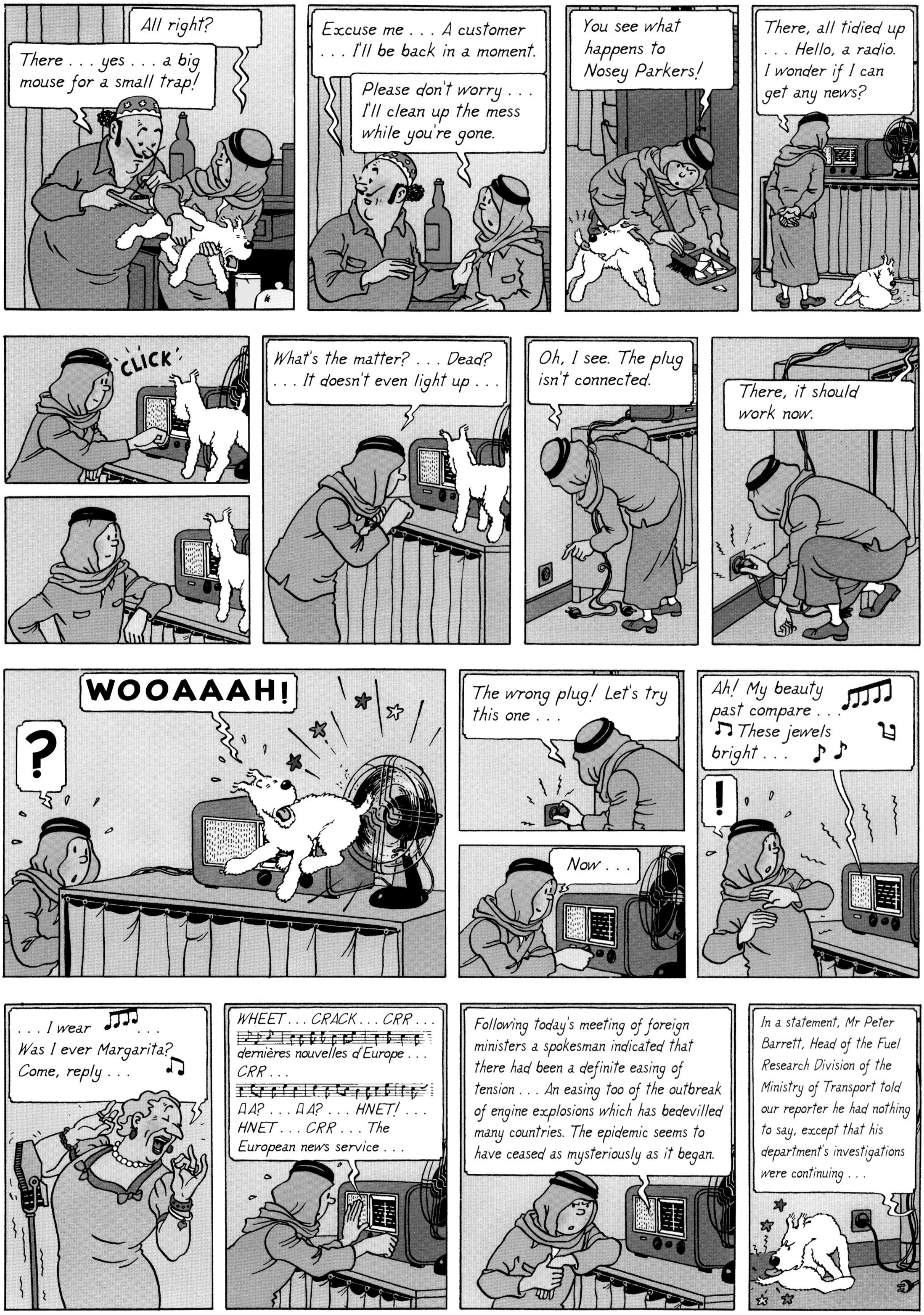
All right?
There . . . yes . . . a big mouse for a small trap!
Excuse me . . . A customer . . . I'll be back in a moment.
Please don't worry . . . I'll clean up the mess while you're gone.
You see what happens to Nosey Parkers!
There, all tidied up . . . Hello, a radio. I wonder if I can get any news?
CLICK
What's the matter? . . . Dead? . . . It doesn't even light up . . .
Oh, I see. The plug isn't connected.
There, it should work now.
WOOAAAH!
?
The wrong plug! Let's try this one . . .
Now . . .
Ah! My beauty past compare . . . These jewels bright . . .
!
. . . I wear . . . Was I ever Margarita? Come, reply . . .
WHEET . . . CRACK . . . CRR . . . dernières nouvelles d'Europe . . . CRR . . . AA? . . . AA? . . . HNET! . . . HNET . . . CRR . . . The European news service . . .
Following today's meeting of foreign ministers a spokesman indicated that there had been a definite easing of tension . . . An easing too of the outbreak of engine explosions which has bedevilled many countries. The epidemic seems to have ceased as mysteriously as it began.
In a statement, Mr Peter Barrett, Head of the Fuel Research Division of the Ministry of Transport told our reporter he had nothing to say, except that his department's investigations were continuing . . .

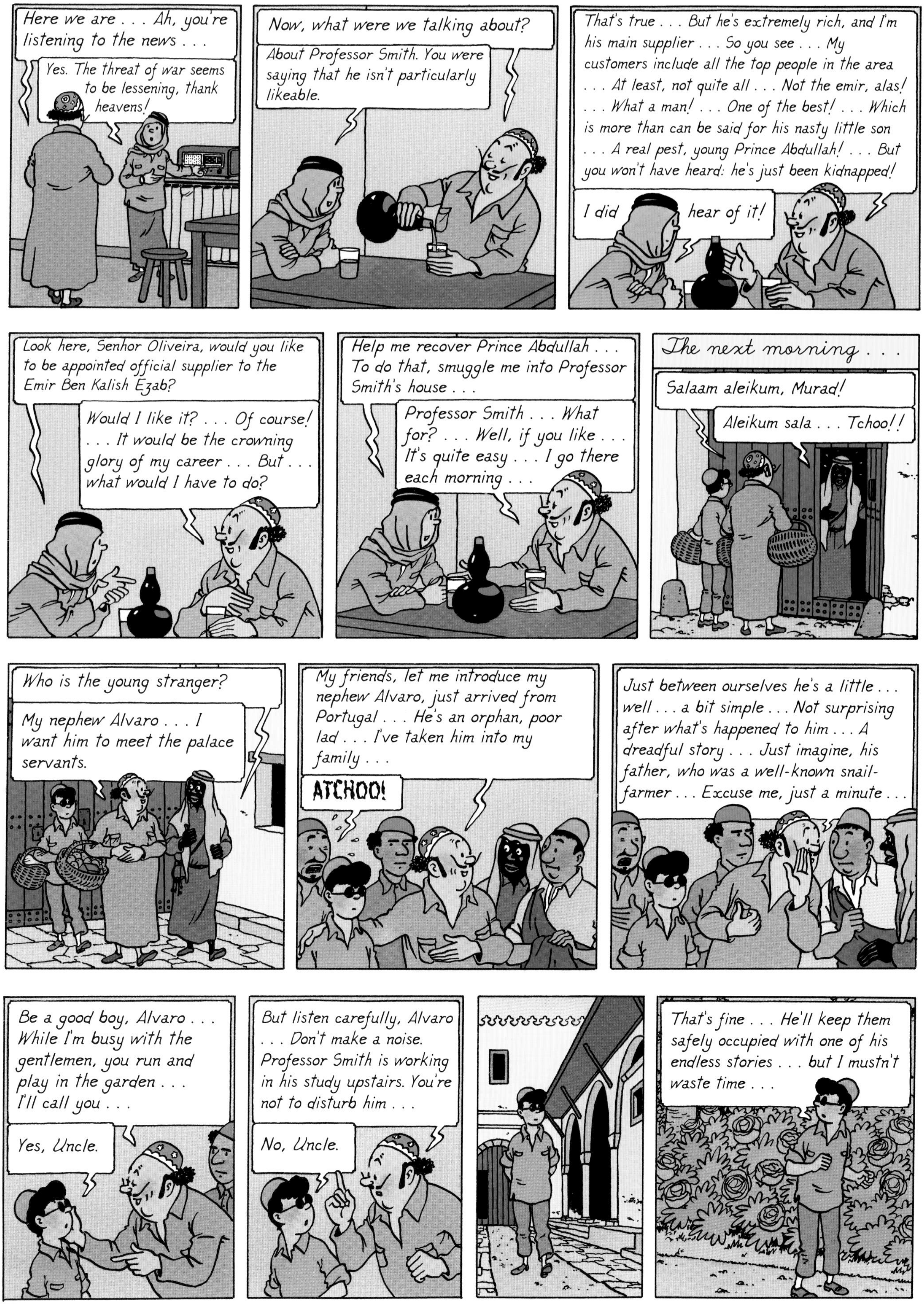
Here we are . . . Ah, you're listening to the news . . .
Yes. The threat of war seems to be lessening, thank heavens!
Now, what were we talking about?
About Professor Smith. You were saying that he isn't particularly likeable.
That's true . . . But he's extremely rich, and I'm his main supplier . . . So you see . . . My customers include all the top people in the area . . . At least, not quite all . . . Not the emir, alas! . . . What a man! . . . One of the best! . . . Which is more than can be said for his nasty little son . . . A real pest, young Prince Abdullah! . . . But you won't have heard: he's just been kidnapped!
I did hear of it!
Look here, Senhor Oliveira, would you like to be appointed official supplier to the Emir Ben Kalish Ezab?
Would I like it? . . . Of course! . . . It would be the crowning glory of my career . . . But . . . what would I have to do?
Help me recover Prince Abdullah . . . To do that, smuggle me into Professor Smith's house . . .
Professor Smith . . . What for? . . . Well, if you like . . . It's quite easy . . . I go there each morning . . .
The next morning . . .
Salaam aleikum, Murad!
Aleikum sala . . . Tchoo!!
Who is the young stranger?
My nephew Alvaro . . . I want him to meet the palace servants.
My friends, let me introduce my nephew Alvaro, just arrived from Portugal . . . He's an orphan, poor lad . . . I've taken him into my family . . .
ATCHOO!
Just between ourselves he's a little . . . well . . . a bit simple . . . Not surprising after what's happened to him . . . A dreadful story . . . Just imagine, his father, who was a well-known snail-farmer . . . Excuse me, just a minute . . .
Be a good boy, Alvaro . . . While I'm busy with the gentlemen, you run and play in the garden . . . I'll call you . . .
Yes, Uncle.
But listen carefully, Alvaro . . . Don't make a noise. Professor Smith is working in his study upstairs. You're not to disturb him . . .
No, Uncle.
That's fine . . . He'll keep them safely occupied with one of his endless stories . . . but I mustn't waste time . . .

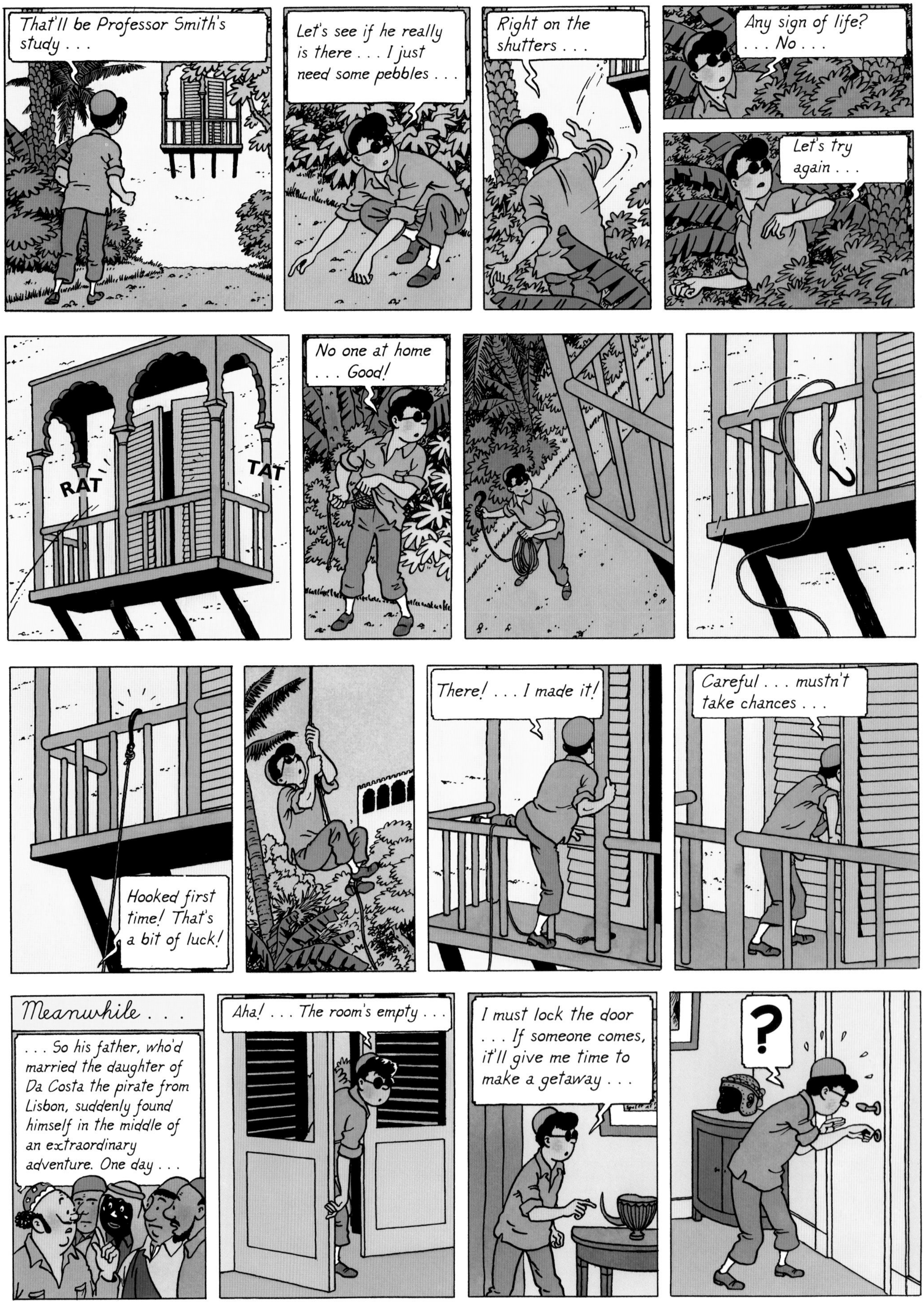

That'll be Professor Smith's study . . .
Let's see if he really is there . . . I just need some pebbles . . .
Right on the shutters . . .
Any sign of life? . . . No . . .
Let's try again . . .
RAT
TAT
No one at home . . . Good!
Hooked first time! That's a bit of luck!
There! . . . I made it!
Careful . . . mustn't take chances . . .
Meanwhile . . .
. . . So his father, who'd married the daughter of Da Costa the pirate from Lisbon, suddenly found himself in the middle of an extraordinary adventure. One day . . .
Aha! . . . The room's empty . . .
I must lock the door . . . If someone comes, it'll give me time to make a getaway . . .
?

The key's in the door ... And the door's locked from the inside! ... But there's no-one here ... It doesn't make sense ...

I'll work that out later ... First, let's have a look at the papers on his desk ...

What's in this folder?

Hello ... A file of newspaper cuttings ...

SCIENT!
BAFFL!

MORE PETROL BLASTS
by our Motoring Corresp...

WORLD'S AIRCRAFT GROUNDED
LONDON, Mond...
Heathrow A...
stan...
tod...
Air...
alme...
depa...
BOA...
and o...
spoke...
passen...

FUEL MYSTERY
What's gone wrong with our petrol?
An outbreak of mysterious automobile explosions is terrorising the world's capitals. Car engines ...

Now why should Dr Müller be interested in that petrol mystery? ... I wonder if ...

ATCHOO!

?!

Great snakes! The hearth is opening! ... I must hide!

Aaah ...

TCHOO!

What's he doing in that corner? ... Ah, I see ... That's where a secret button for the trapdoor must be hidden.

Aaah ... Aaah ... TCHOO! ... Aaah ... TCHOO! ... Ach, that little pest! ...

Lucky I persuaded him to swap his confounded box of sneezing powder for a pair of roller-skates ...

There ... I'll burn it in a minute ...

Drat! He's starting to write!

Let's hope he won't be long ... I'm beginning to get pins and needles ...

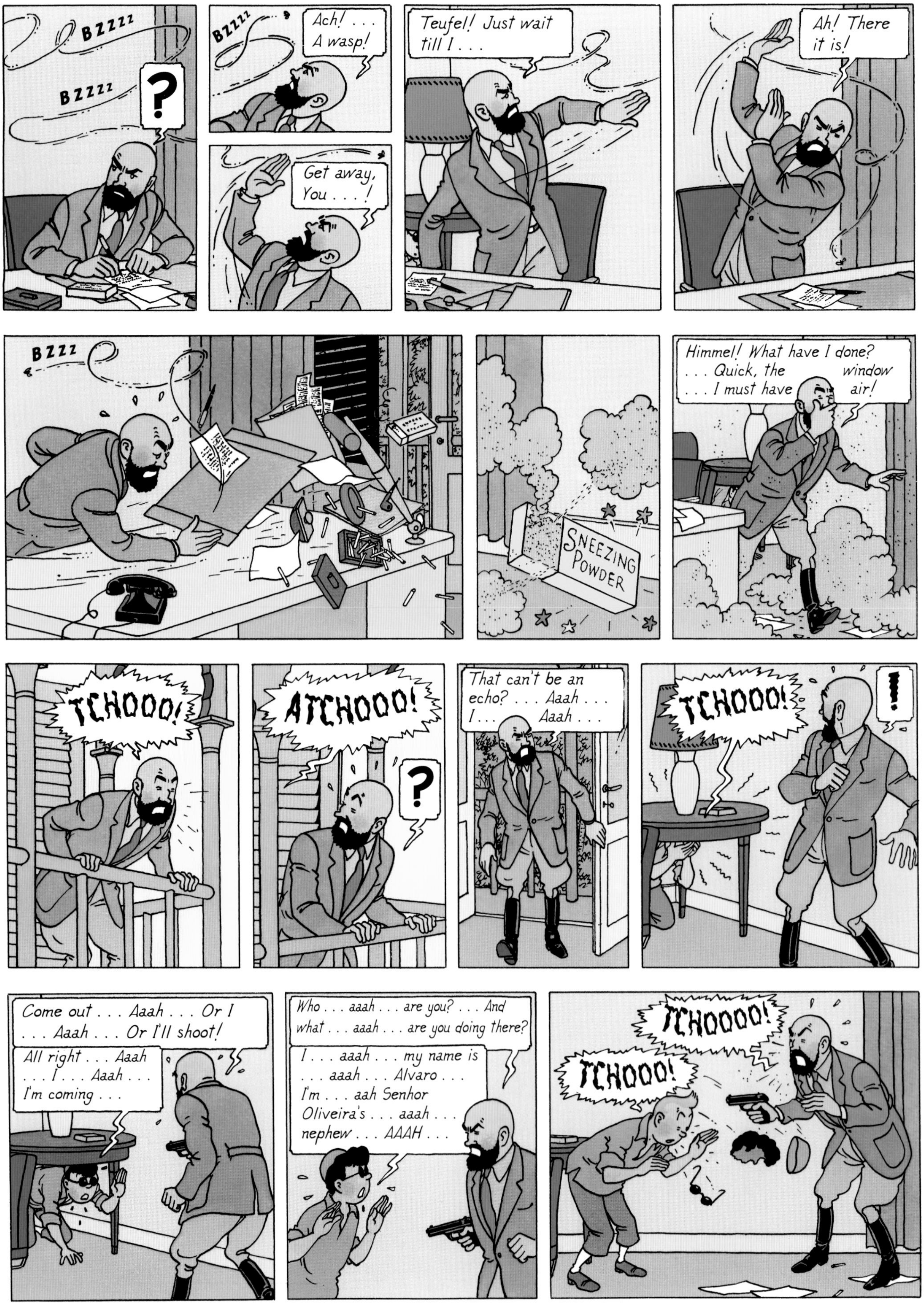

BZZZZ
BZZZZ
?
BZZZZ
Ach! . . . A wasp!
Get away, You . . . !
Teufel! Just wait till I . . .
Ah! There it is!
BZZZ
SNEEZING POWDER
Himmel! What have I done? . . . Quick, the window . . . I must have air!
TCHOOO!
ATCHOOO!
?
That can't be an echo? . . . Aaah . . . I . . . Aaah . . .
TCHOOO!
!
Come out . . . Aaah . . . Or I . . . Aaah . . . Or I'll shoot!
All right . . . Aaah . . . I . . . Aaah . . . I'm coming . . .
Who . . . aaah . . . are you? . . . And what . . . aaah . . . are you doing there?
I . . . aaah . . . my name is . . . aaah . . . Alvaro . . . I'm . . . aah Senhor Oliveira's . . . aaah . . . nephew . . . AAAH . . .
TCHOOOO!
TCHOOO!

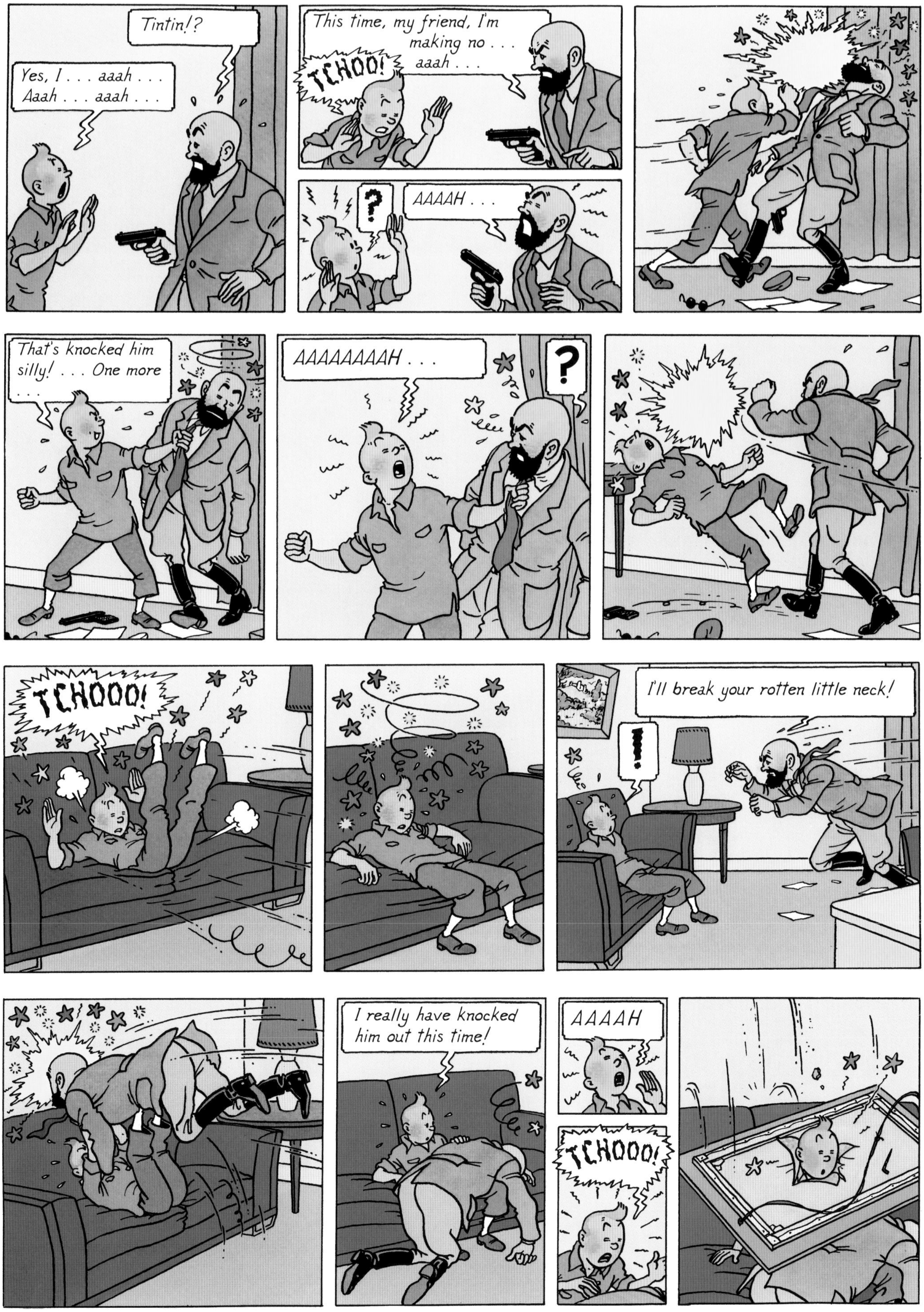
Tintin!?
Yes, I . . . aaah . . . Aaah . . . aaah . . .
This time, my friend, I'm making no . . . aaah . . .
TCHOO!
?
AAAAH . . .
That's knocked him silly! . . . One more . . .
AAAAAAAAH . . .
?
TCHOOO!
I'll break your rotten little neck!
!
I really have knocked him out this time!
AAAAH
TCHOOO!

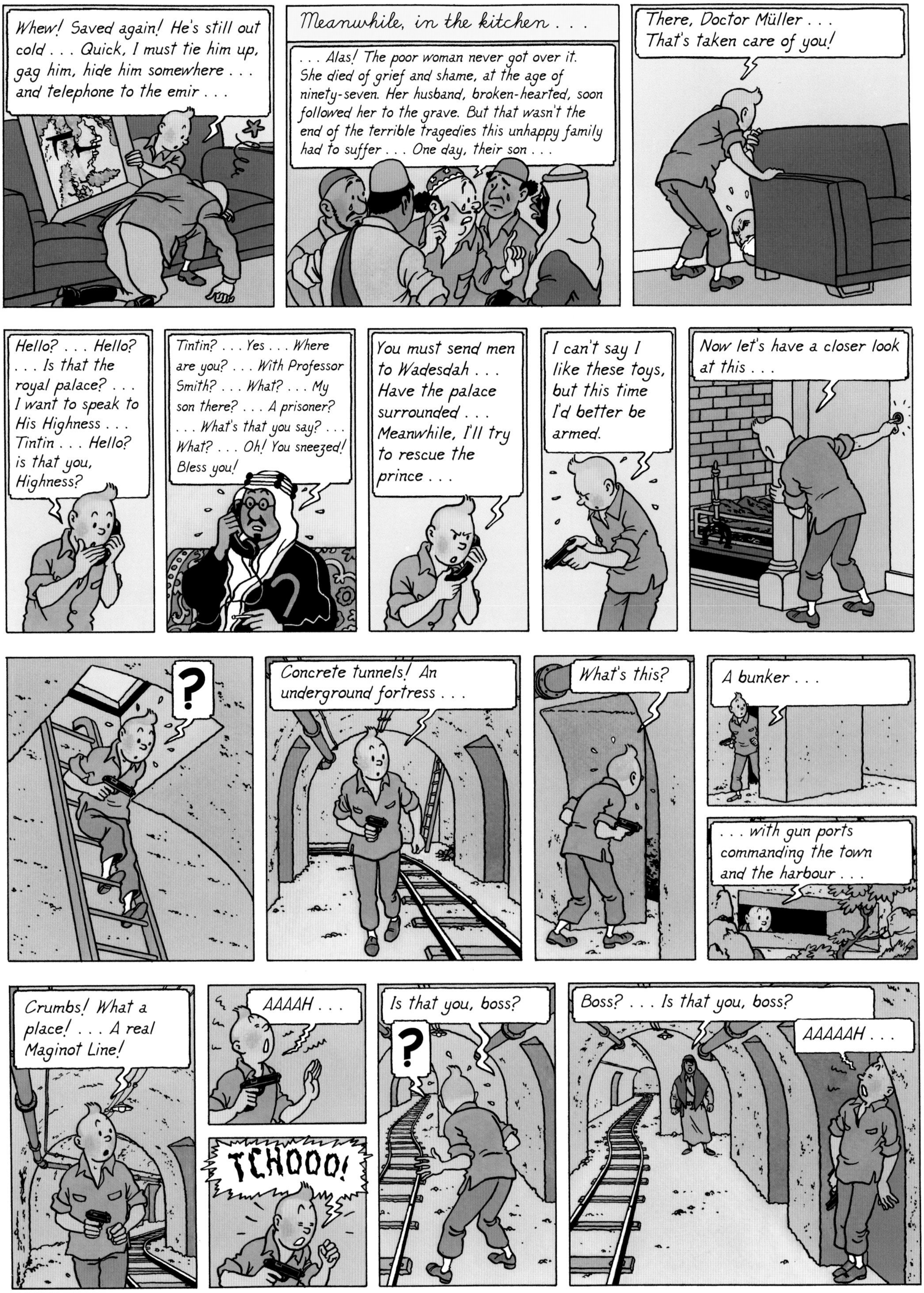
Whew! Saved again! He's still out cold . . . Quick, I must tie him up, gag him, hide him somewhere . . . and telephone to the emir . . .
Meanwhile, in the kitchen . . .
. . . Alas! The poor woman never got over it. She died of grief and shame, at the age of ninety-seven. Her husband, broken-hearted, soon followed her to the grave. But that wasn't the end of the terrible tragedies this unhappy family had to suffer . . . One day, their son . . .
There, Doctor Müller . . . That's taken care of you!
Hello? . . . Hello? . . . Is that the royal palace? . . . I want to speak to His Highness . . . Tintin . . . Hello? is that you, Highness?
Tintin? . . . Yes . . . Where are you? . . . With Professor Smith? . . . What? . . . My son there? . . . A prisoner? . . . What's that you say? . . . What? . . . Oh! You sneezed! Bless you!
You must send men to Wadesdah . . . Have the palace surrounded . . . Meanwhile, I'll try to rescue the prince . . .
I can't say I like these toys, but this time I'd better be armed.
Now let's have a closer look at this . . .
?
Concrete tunnels! An underground fortress . . .
What's this?
A bunker . . .
. . . with gun ports commanding the town and the harbour . . .
Crumbs! What a place! . . . A real Maginot Line!
AAAAH . . .
TCHOOO!
Is that you, boss?
?
Boss? . . . Is that you, boss?
AAAAAH . . .

Nobody there . . . that's odd . . .

I could have sworn I heard a sneeze . . .

Stop! . . . Hands up . . . or I'll shoot! . . .

!

Don't move, and don't make a sound . . . or else . . .

Right! . . . Now you're going to take me to the emir's son . . . Get moving, and don't try any funny business! . . . Understand?

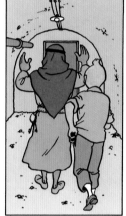

He's in there . . .

You've got the key? . . . Open up . . .

All right? . . . Stand away . . . Face the wall, and keep your hands up . . .

Quick, Abdullah! . . . Hurry! . . . I've come to take you home to your father . . .

Shan't! . . . Don't want to go home! . . . This is a nice game . . . Let me go! . . . I hate you! . . . I won't go!

But . . .

BANG

Abdullah! . . . Come along Abdullah! . . . There isn't time to play about . . .

?

اترك هذا

49

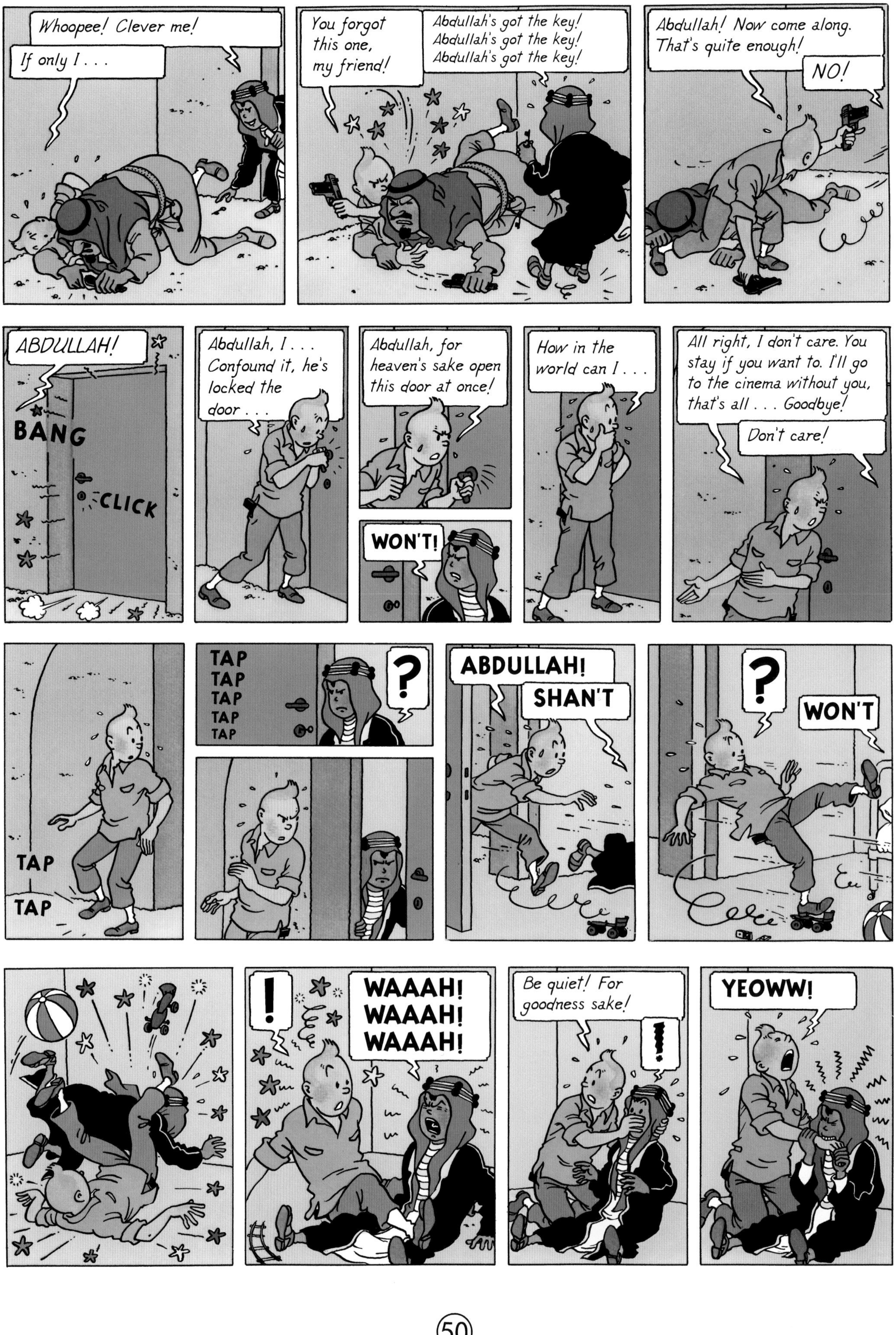

If only I . . .
Whoopee! Clever me!
You forgot this one, my friend!
Abdullah's got the key! Abdullah's got the key! Abdullah's got the key!
Abdullah! Now come along. That's quite enough!
NO!
ABDULLAH!
BANG
CLICK
Abdullah, I . . . Confound it, he's locked the door . . .
Abdullah, for heaven's sake open this door at once!
WON'T!
How in the world can I . . .
All right, I don't care. You stay if you want to. I'll go to the cinema without you, that's all . . . Goodbye!
Don't care!
TAP
TAP
TAP TAP TAP TAP TAP
?
ABDULLAH!
SHAN'T
?
WON'T
!
WAAAH! WAAAH! WAAAH!
Be quiet! For goodness sake!
YEOWW!

Be quiet, you little pest! Be quiet!

SHAN'T

WAAAH! WAAAH! WAAAH!

What about him? . . . I ought to tie him up, but . . .

WAAAH!

WAAAH! WAAAH!

CLICK

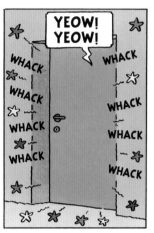

YEOW! YEOW!

WHACK WHACK
WHACK WHACK
WHACK WHACK
WHACK WHACK
WHACK WHACK

I hate you! . . . I shall tell my papa! . . . And my papa is the emir! . . .

Oh yes . . .

Great snakes! He's come round . . . He'll raise the alarm, that's for sure . . .

?

. . . And my papa will have you flogged . . . And then he'll have you impaled . . .

Good idea . . .

Quick, Murad! . . . Find Daud and Abdul . . . Take Daud with you and start searching from the far end . . . Send Abdul to me . . . We'll wait here for the young swine . . .

I go, master.

. . . At that moment the count stepped forward. Aha! he cried in Portuguese (you mustn't forget, Portuguese was his native tongue) and without a moment's hesitation he flung open the door . . . He stood frozen with horror! . . .

Daud! . . . Abdul! . . . Come at once! . . . The master needs you!

I . . . er . . . how I rattle on! I must go . . . an important appointment . . . Er . . . if you see my nephew, send him home, will you? . . . Goodbye!

With us here and Murad and Daud at the other end, he's trapped!

. . . And then he'll cut off your head . . . and play skittles with it . . . So there!

He can't escape . . . with the boss guarding the other exit . . .

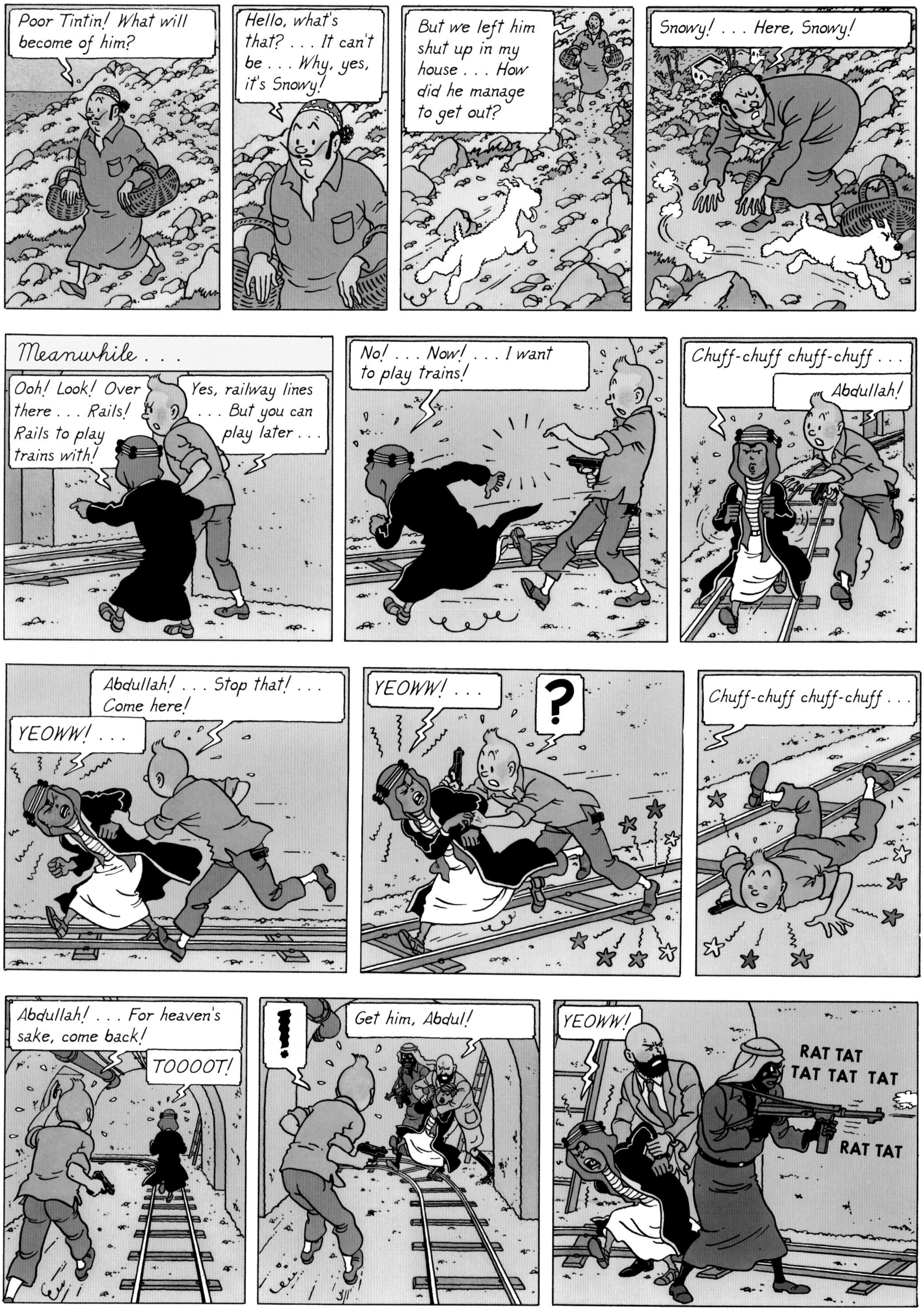
Poor Tintin! What will become of him?
Hello, what's that? . . . It can't be . . . Why, yes, it's Snowy!
But we left him shut up in my house . . . How did he manage to get out?
Snowy! . . . Here, Snowy!
Meanwhile . . .
Ooh! Look! Over there . . . Rails! Rails to play trains with!
Yes, railway lines . . . But you can play later . . .
No! . . . Now! . . . I want to play trains!
Chuff-chuff chuff-chuff . . .
Abdullah!
Abdullah! . . . Stop that! . . . Come here!
YEOWW! . . .
YEOWW! . . .
?
Chuff-chuff chuff-chuff . . .
Abdullah! . . . For heaven's sake, come back!
TOOOOT!
!
Get him, Abdul!
YEOWW!
RAT TAT
TAT TAT TAT
RAT TAT

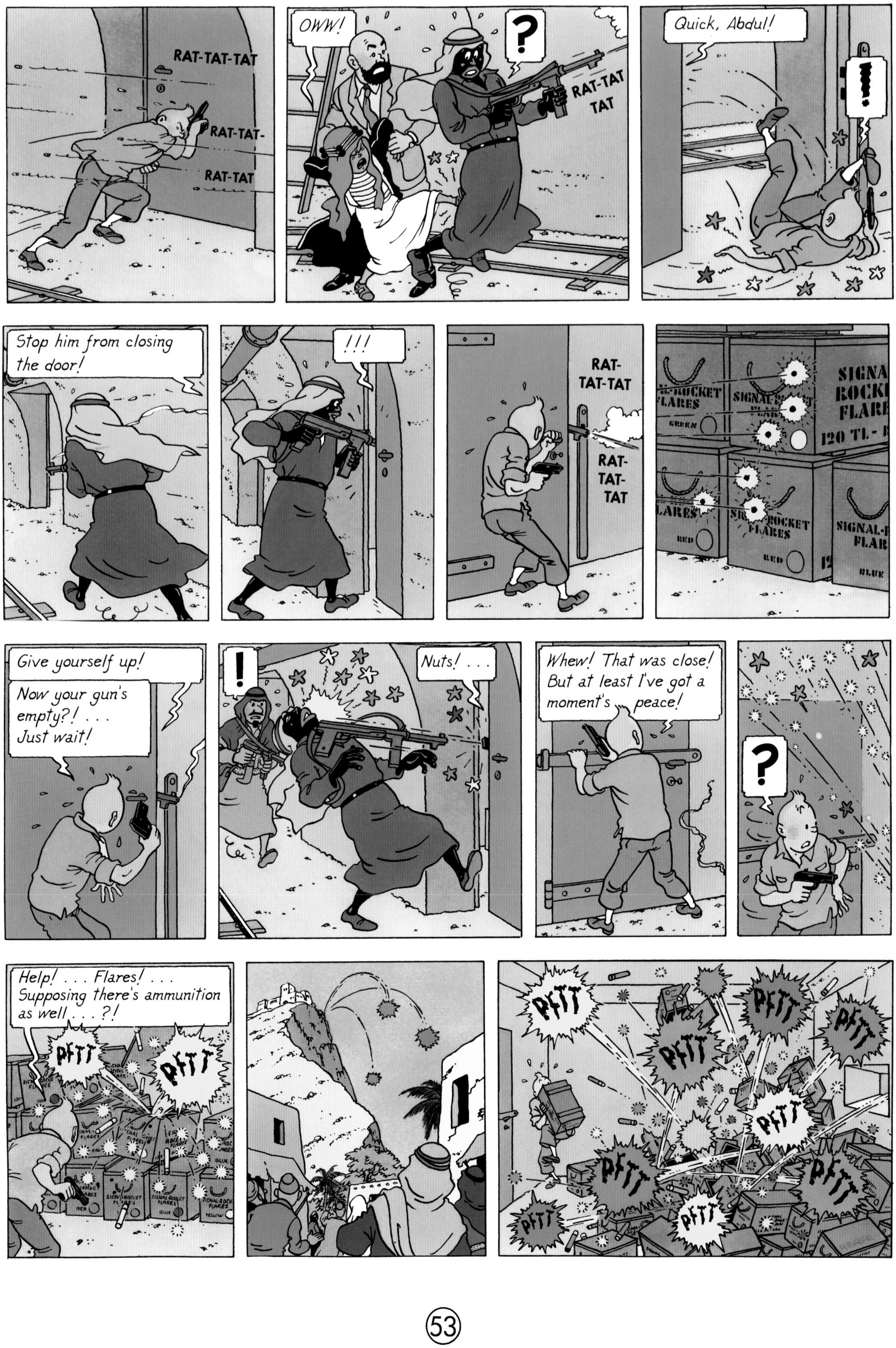

RAT-TAT-TAT
RAT-TAT-
RAT-TAT
OWW!
?
RAT-TAT TAT
Quick, Abdul!
!
Stop him from closing the door!
!!!
RAT-TAT-TAT
RAT-TAT-TAT
SIGNAL ROCKET FLARES
120 TL
ROCKET FLARES
GREEN
FLARES
RED
SIGNAL-ROCKET FLARES
ROCKET FLARES
BLUE
Give yourself up!
Now your gun's empty?! . . . Just wait!
!
Nuts! . . .
Whew! That was close! But at least I've got a moment's peace!
?
Help! . . . Flares! . . . Supposing there's ammunition as well . . . ?!
PFTT
PFTT
PFTT
PFTT
PFTT
PFTT
PFTT
PFTT
PFTT
PFTT
PFTT

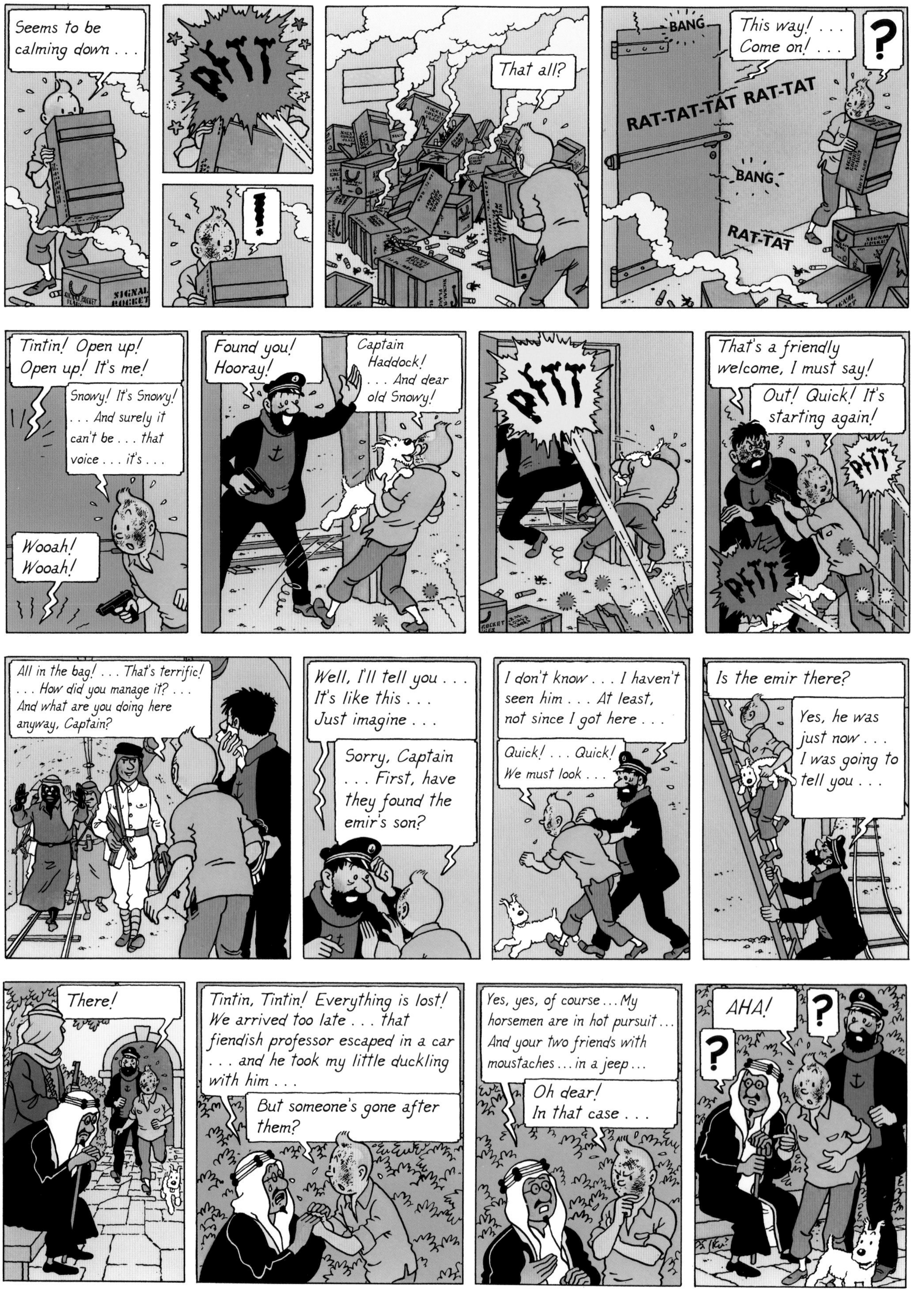
Seems to be calming down . . .
PFTT
!
That all?
BANG
This way! . . . Come on! . . .
?
RAT-TAT-TAT RAT-TAT
BANG
RAT-TAT
Tintin! Open up! Open up! It's me!
Snowy! It's Snowy! . . . And surely it can't be . . . that voice . . . it's . . .
Wooah! Wooah!
Found you! Hooray!
Captain Haddock! . . . And dear old Snowy!
PFTT
That's a friendly welcome, I must say!
Out! Quick! It's starting again!
PFTT
PFTT
All in the bag! . . . That's terrific! . . . How did you manage it? . . . And what are you doing here anyway, Captain?
Well, I'll tell you . . . It's like this . . . Just imagine . . .
Sorry, Captain . . . First, have they found the emir's son?
I don't know . . . I haven't seen him . . . At least, not since I got here . . .
Quick! . . . Quick! We must look . . .
Is the emir there?
Yes, he was just now . . . I was going to tell you . . .
There!
Tintin, Tintin! Everything is lost! We arrived too late . . . that fiendish professor escaped in a car . . . and he took my little duckling with him . . .
But someone's gone after them?
Yes, yes, of course . . . My horsemen are in hot pursuit . . . And your two friends with moustaches . . . in a jeep . . .
Oh dear! In that case . . .
AHA!
?
?

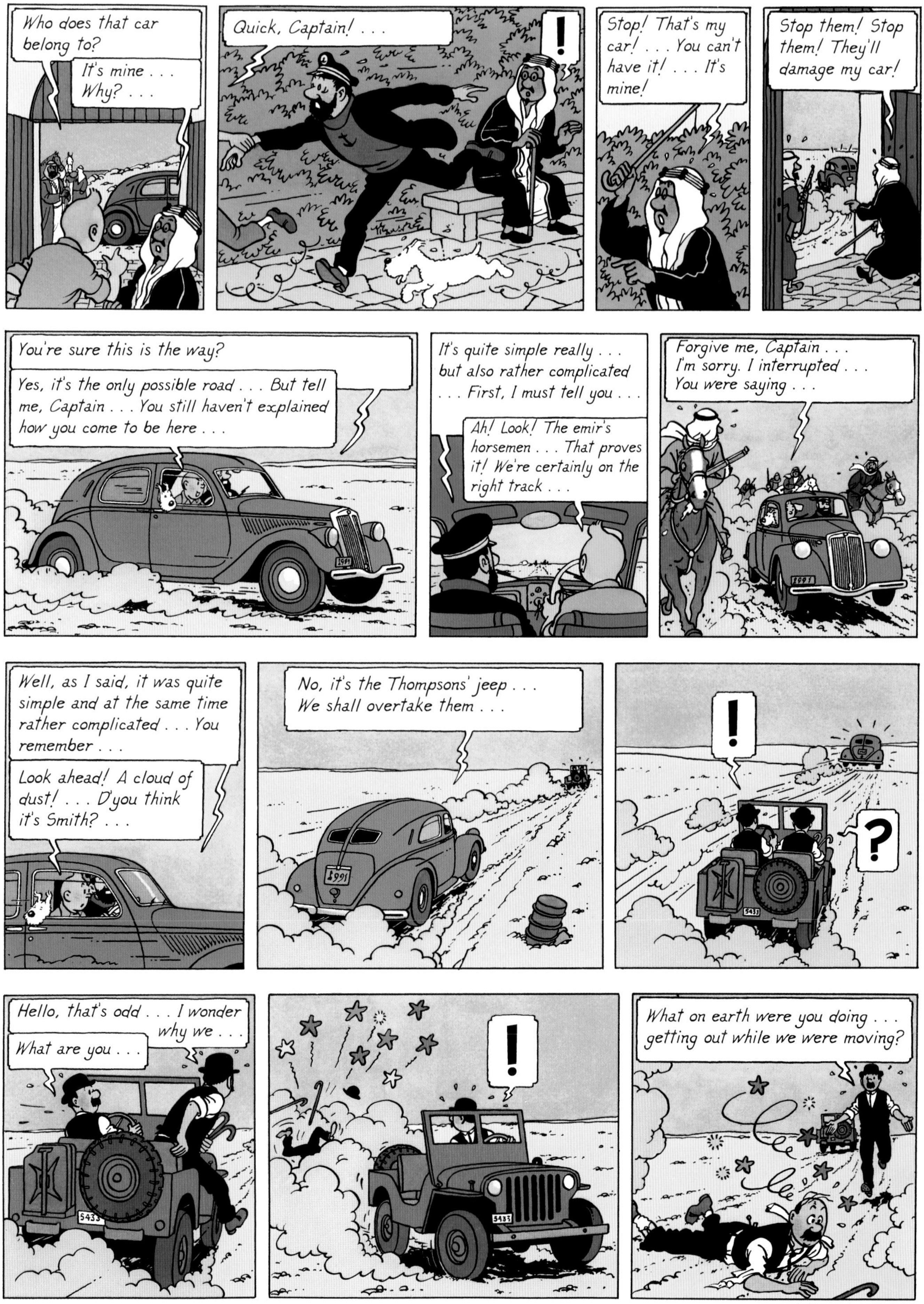
Who does that car belong to?
It's mine . . . Why? . . .
Quick, Captain! . . .
!
Stop! That's my car! . . . You can't have it! . . . It's mine!
Stop them! Stop them! They'll damage my car!
You're sure this is the way?
Yes, it's the only possible road . . . But tell me, Captain . . . You still haven't explained how you come to be here . . .
It's quite simple really . . . but also rather complicated . . . First, I must tell you . . .
Ah! Look! The emir's horsemen . . . That proves it! We're certainly on the right track . . .
Forgive me, Captain . . . I'm sorry. I interrupted . . . You were saying . . .
Well, as I said, it was quite simple and at the same time rather complicated . . . You remember . . .
Look ahead! A cloud of dust! . . . D'you think it's Smith? . . .
No, it's the Thompsons' jeep . . . We shall overtake them . . .
!
?
Hello, that's odd . . . I wonder why we . . .
What are you . . .
!
What on earth were you doing . . . getting out while we were moving?

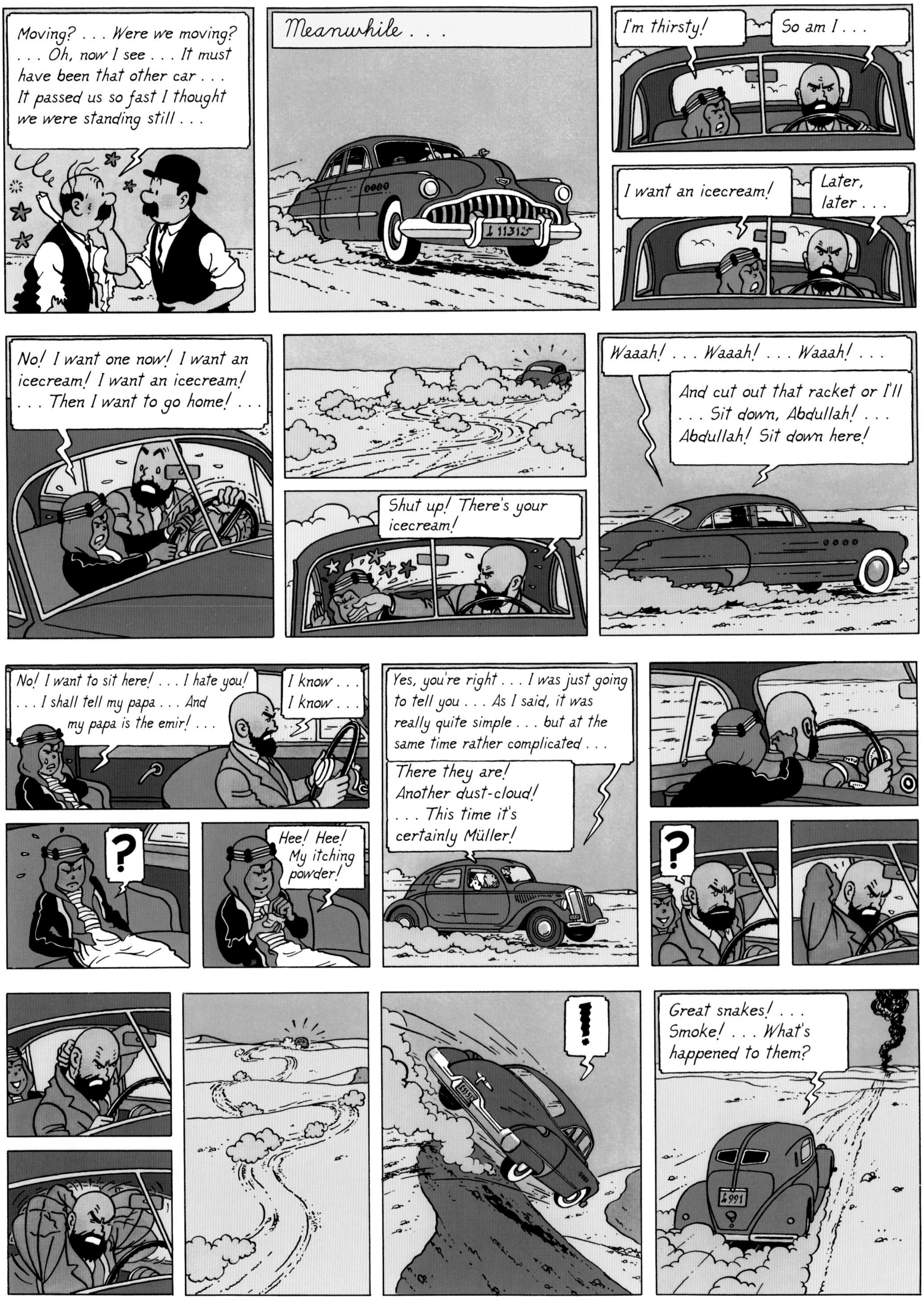
Moving? . . . Were we moving? . . . Oh, now I see . . . It must have been that other car . . . It passed us so fast I thought we were standing still . . .
Meanwhile . . .
I'm thirsty!
So am I . . .
I want an icecream!
Later, later . . .
No! I want one now! I want an icecream! I want an icecream! . . . Then I want to go home! . . .
Shut up! There's your icecream!
Waaah! . . . Waaah! . . . Waaah! . . .
And cut out that racket or I'll . . . Sit down, Abdullah! . . . Abdullah! Sit down here!
No! I want to sit here! . . . I hate you! . . . I shall tell my papa . . . And my papa is the emir! . . .
I know . . . I know . . .
Yes, you're right . . . I was just going to tell you . . . As I said, it was really quite simple . . . but at the same time rather complicated . . .
There they are! Another dust-cloud! . . . This time it's certainly Müller!
?
Hee! Hee! My itching powder!
?
!
Great snakes! . . . Smoke! . . . What's happened to them?

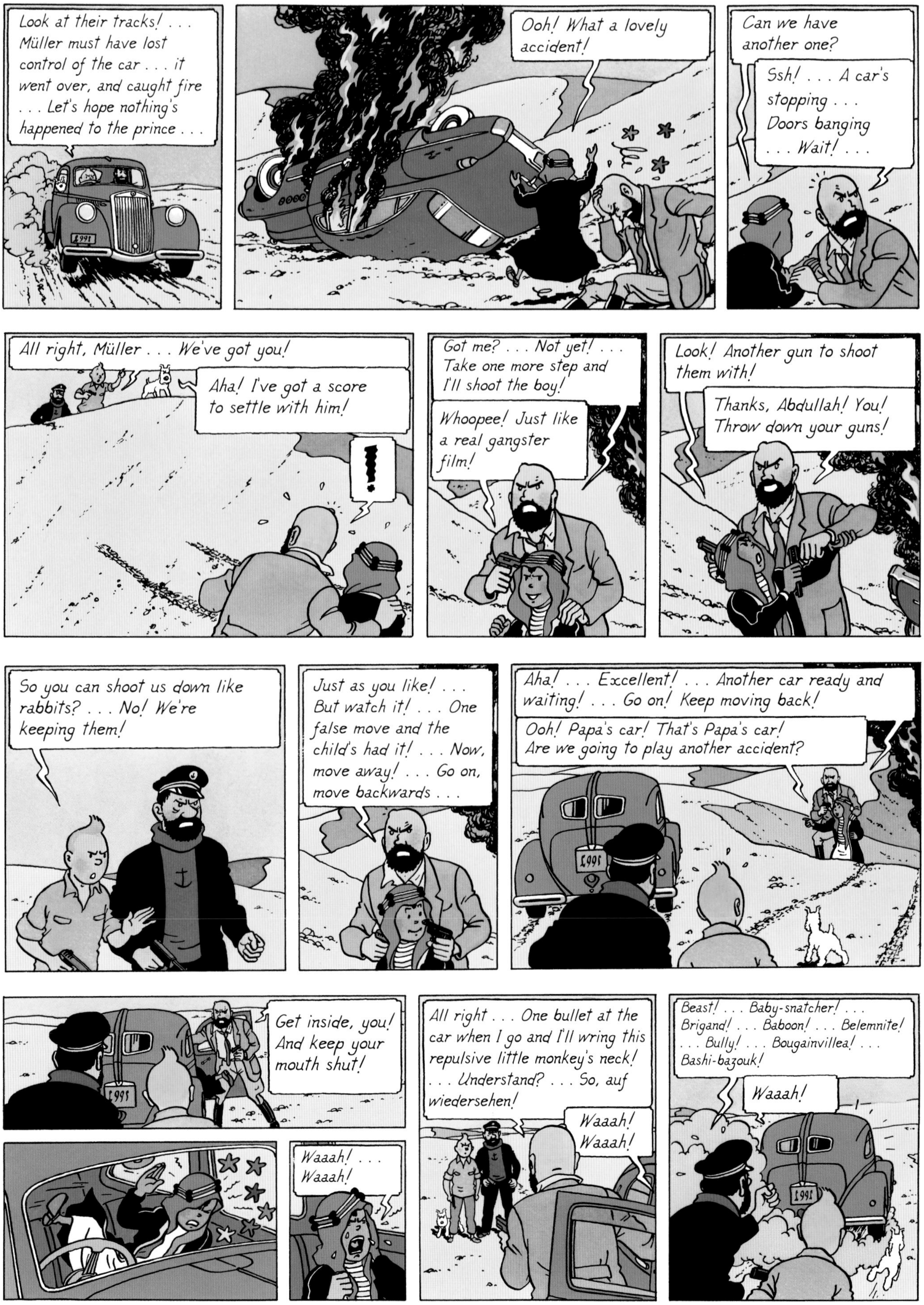
Look at their tracks! . . . Müller must have lost control of the car . . . it went over, and caught fire . . . Let's hope nothing's happened to the prince . . .
Ooh! What a lovely accident!
Can we have another one?
Ssh! . . . A car's stopping . . . Doors banging . . . Wait! . . .
All right, Müller . . . We've got you!
Aha! I've got a score to settle with him!
!!!
Got me? . . . Not yet! . . . Take one more step and I'll shoot the boy!
Whoopee! Just like a real gangster film!
Look! Another gun to shoot them with!
Thanks, Abdullah! You! Throw down your guns!
So you can shoot us down like rabbits? . . . No! We're keeping them!
Just as you like! . . . But watch it! . . . One false move and the child's had it! . . . Now, move away! . . . Go on, move backwards . . .
Aha! . . . Excellent! . . . Another car ready and waiting! . . . Go on! Keep moving back!
Ooh! Papa's car! That's Papa's car! Are we going to play another accident?
Get inside, you! And keep your mouth shut!
Waaah! . . . Waaah!
All right . . . One bullet at the car when I go and I'll wring this repulsive little monkey's neck! . . . Understand? . . . So, auf wiedersehen!
Waaah! Waaah!
Beast! . . . Baby-snatcher! . . . Brigand! . . . Baboon! . . . Belemnite! . . . Bully! . . . Bougainvillea! . . . Bashi-bazouk!
Waaah!

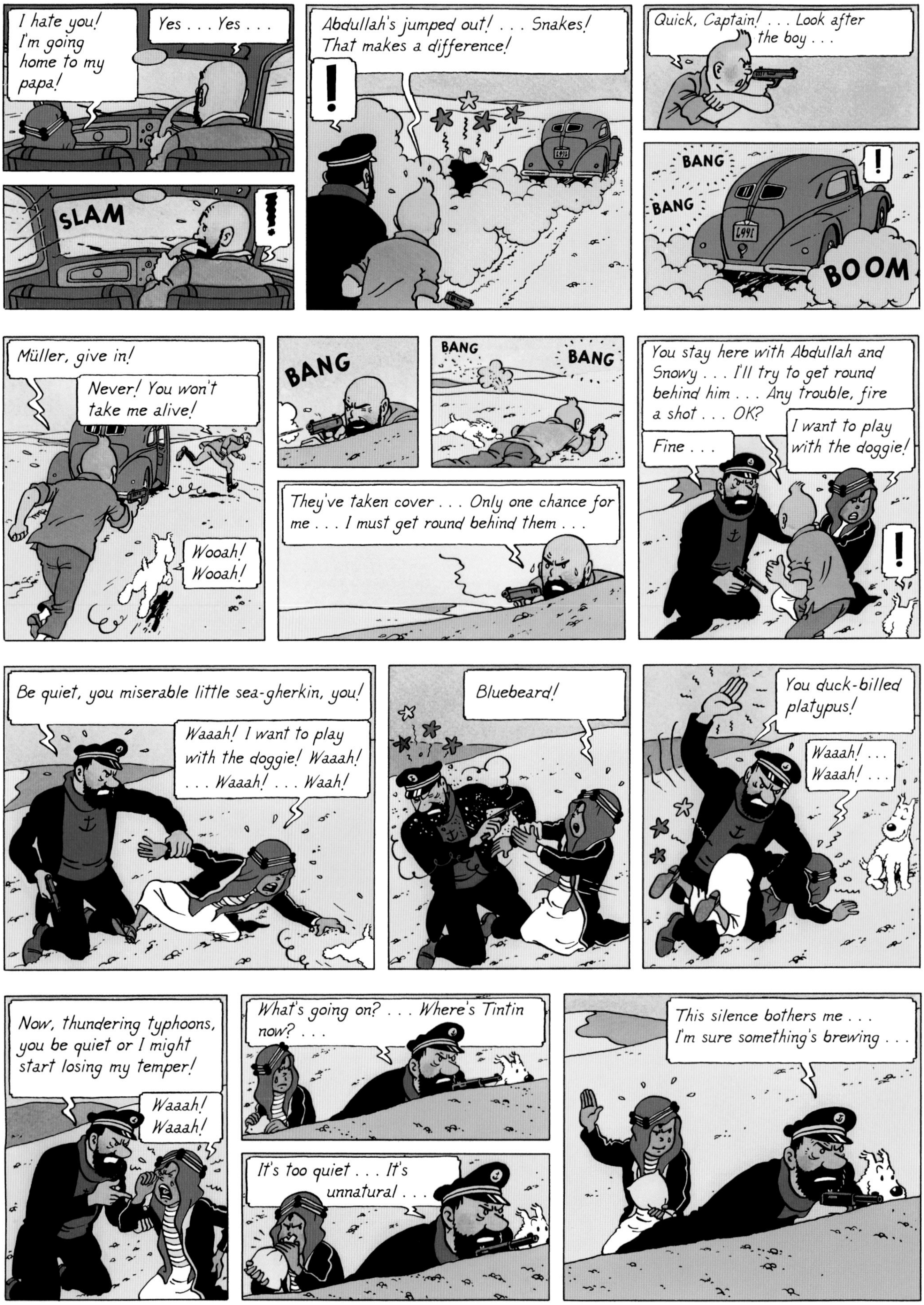

I hate you! I'm going home to my papa!
Yes . . . Yes . . .
SLAM
Abdullah's jumped out! . . . Snakes! That makes a difference!
Quick, Captain! . . . Look after the boy . . .
BANG
BANG
BOOM
Müller, give in!
Never! You won't take me alive!
Wooah! Wooah!
BANG
BANG
BANG
They've taken cover . . . Only one chance for me . . . I must get round behind them . . .
You stay here with Abdullah and Snowy . . . I'll try to get round behind him . . . Any trouble, fire a shot . . . OK?
Fine . . .
I want to play with the doggie!
Be quiet, you miserable little sea-gherkin, you!
Waaah! I want to play with the doggie! Waaah! . . . Waaah! . . . Waah!
Bluebeard!
You duck-billed platypus!
Waaah! . . . Waaah! . . .
Now, thundering typhoons, you be quiet or I might start losing my temper!
Waaah! Waaah!
What's going on? . . . Where's Tintin now? . . .
It's too quiet . . . It's unnatural . . .
This silence bothers me . . . I'm sure something's brewing . . .

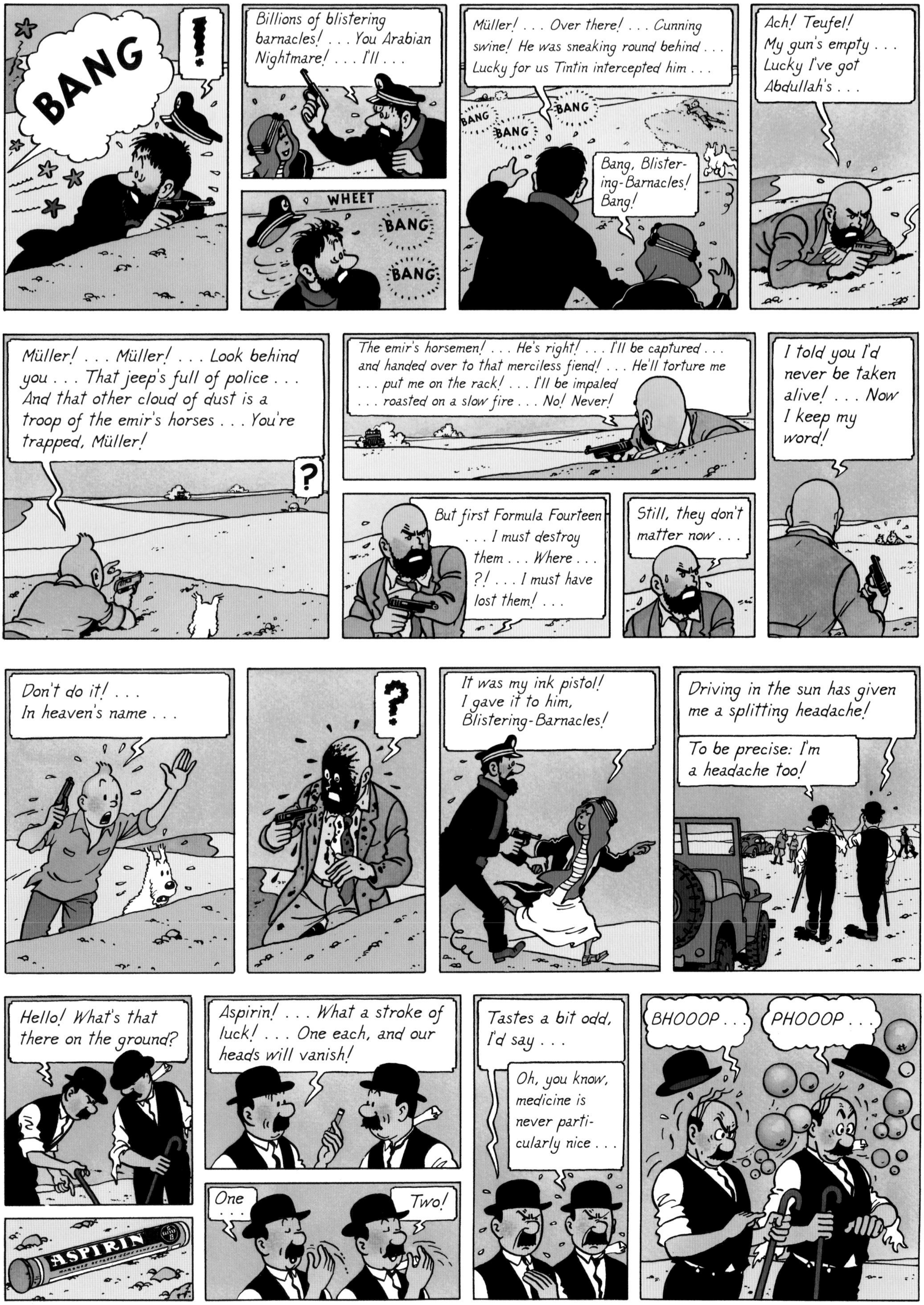
BANG
!
Billions of blistering barnacles! . . . You Arabian Nightmare! . . . I'll . . .
WHEET
BANG
BANG
Müller! . . . Over there! . . . Cunning swine! He was sneaking round behind . . . Lucky for us Tintin intercepted him . . .
BANG
BANG
BANG
Bang, Blistering-Barnacles! Bang!
Ach! Teufel! My gun's empty . . . Lucky I've got Abdullah's . . .
Müller! . . . Müller! . . . Look behind you . . . That jeep's full of police . . . And that other cloud of dust is a troop of the emir's horses . . . You're trapped, Müller!
?
The emir's horsemen! . . . He's right! . . . I'll be captured . . . and handed over to that merciless fiend! . . . He'll torture me . . . put me on the rack! . . . I'll be impaled . . . roasted on a slow fire . . . No! Never!
But first Formula Fourteen . . . I must destroy them . . . Where . . . ?! . . . I must have lost them! . . .
Still, they don't matter now . . .
I told you I'd never be taken alive! . . . Now I keep my word!
Don't do it! . . . In heaven's name . . .
?
It was my ink pistol! I gave it to him, Blistering-Barnacles!
Driving in the sun has given me a splitting headache!
To be precise: I'm a headache too!
Hello! What's that there on the ground?
ASPIRIN
Aspirin! . . . What a stroke of luck! . . . One each, and our heads will vanish!
One . . .
Two!
Tastes a bit odd, I'd say . . .
Oh, you know, medicine is never particularly nice . . .
BHOOOP . . .
PHOOOP . . .

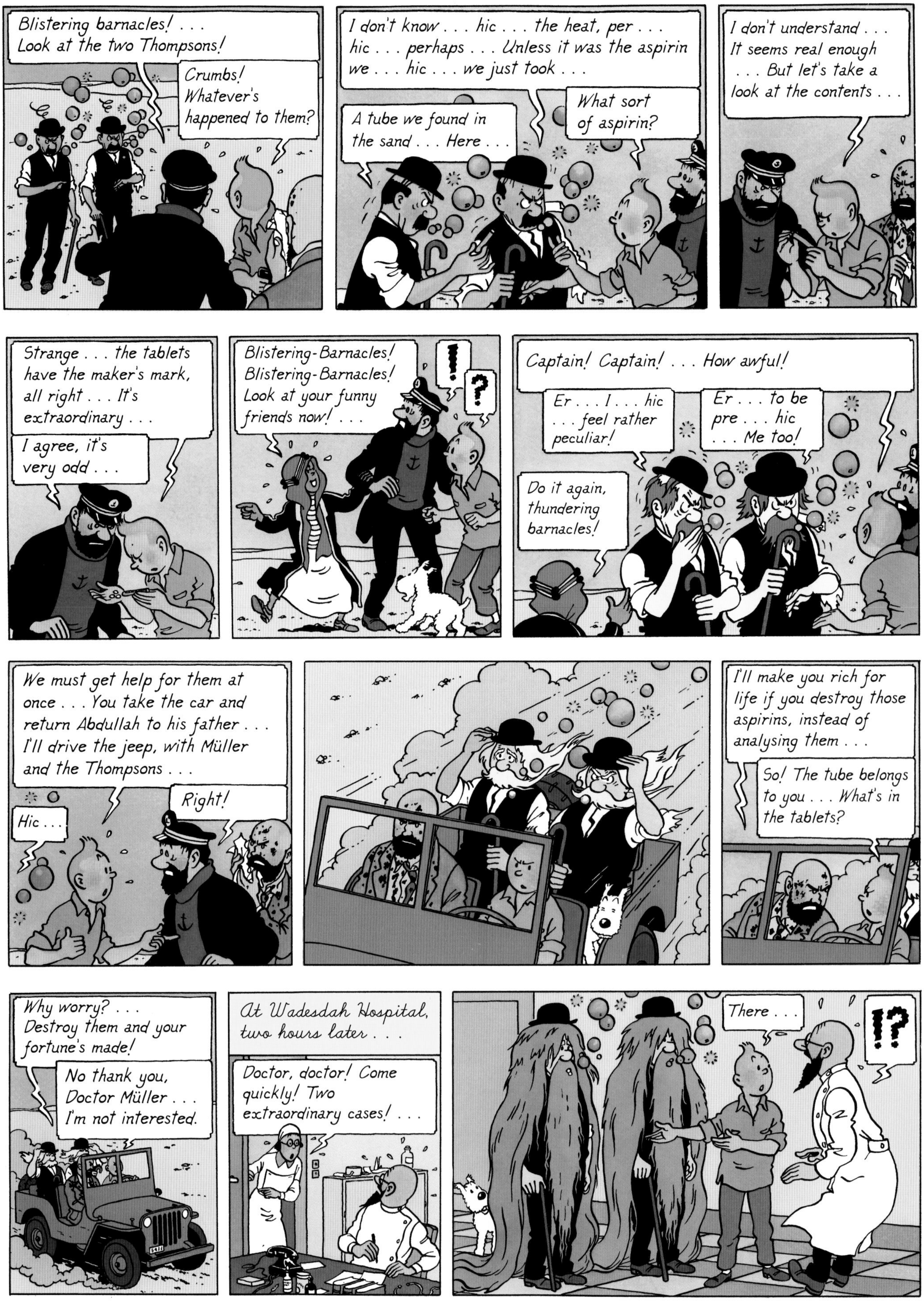
Blistering barnacles! . . . Look at the two Thompsons!
Crumbs! Whatever's happened to them?
I don't know . . . hic . . . the heat, per . . . hic . . . perhaps . . . Unless it was the aspirin we . . . hic . . . we just took . . .
A tube we found in the sand . . . Here . . .
What sort of aspirin?
I don't understand . . . It seems real enough . . . But let's take a look at the contents . . .
Strange . . . the tablets have the maker's mark, all right . . . It's extraordinary . . .
I agree, it's very odd . . .
Blistering-Barnacles! Blistering-Barnacles! Look at your funny friends now! . . .
!
?
Captain! Captain! . . . How awful!
Er . . . I . . . hic . . . feel rather peculiar!
Er . . . to be pre . . . hic . . . Me too!
Do it again, thundering barnacles!
We must get help for them at once . . . You take the car and return Abdullah to his father . . . I'll drive the jeep, with Müller and the Thompsons . . .
Hic . . .
Right!
I'll make you rich for life if you destroy those aspirins, instead of analysing them . . .
So! The tube belongs to you . . . What's in the tablets?
Why worry? . . . Destroy them and your fortune's made!
No thank you, Doctor Müller . . . I'm not interested.
At Wadesdah Hospital, two hours later . . .
Doctor, doctor! Come quickly! Two extraordinary cases! . . .
There . . .
!?

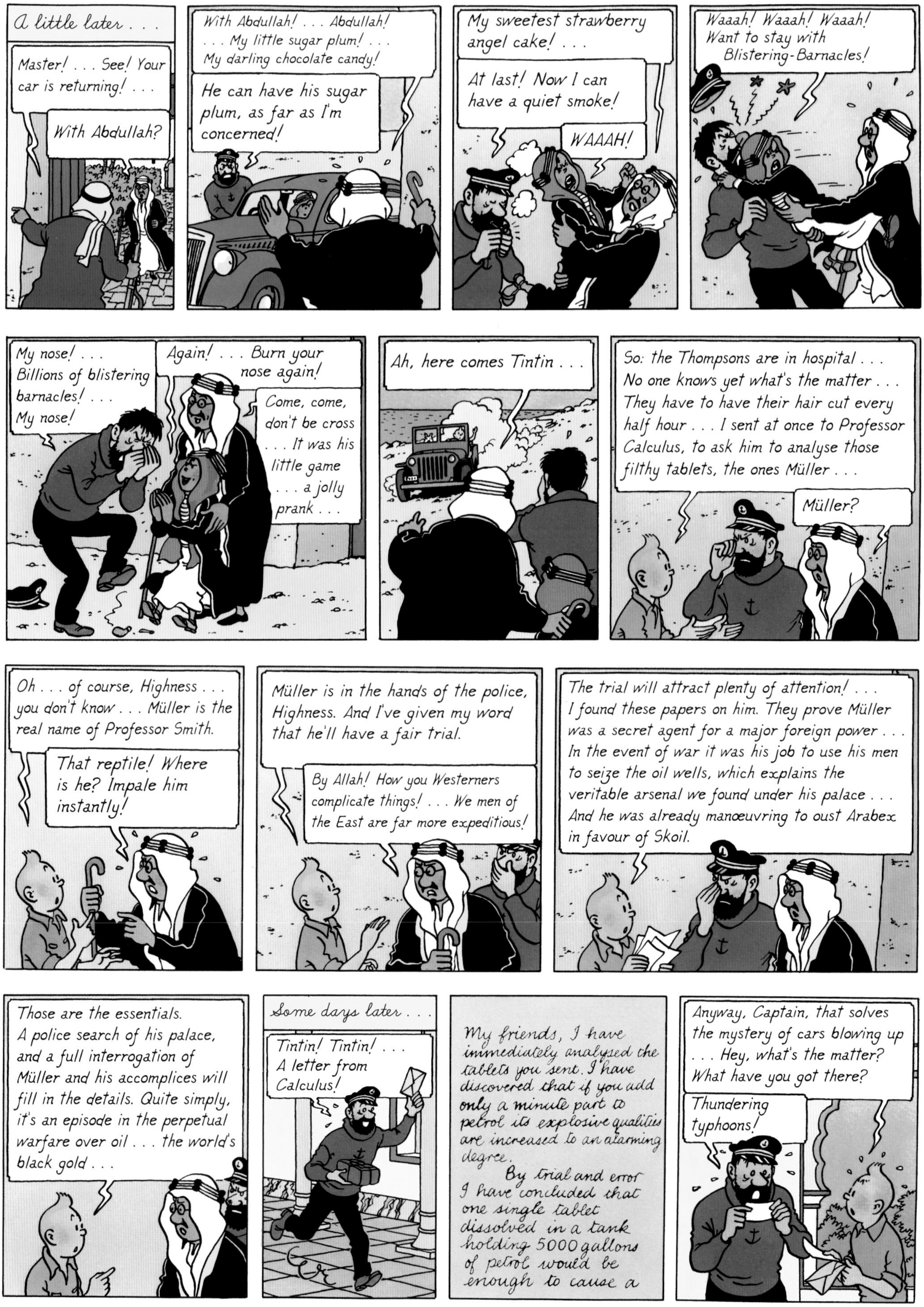
A little later . . .
Master! . . . See! Your car is returning! . . .
With Abdullah?
With Abdullah! . . . Abdullah! . . . My little sugar plum! . . . My darling chocolate candy!
He can have his sugar plum, as far as I'm concerned!
My sweetest strawberry angel cake! . . .
At last! Now I can have a quiet smoke!
WAAAH!
Waaah! Waaah! Waaah! Want to stay with Blistering-Barnacles!
My nose! . . . Billions of blistering barnacles! . . . My nose!
Again! . . . Burn your nose again!
Come, come, don't be cross . . . It was his little game . . . a jolly prank . . .
Ah, here comes Tintin . . .
So: the Thompsons are in hospital . . . No one knows yet what's the matter . . . They have to have their hair cut every half hour . . . I sent at once to Professor Calculus, to ask him to analyse those filthy tablets, the ones Müller . . .
Müller?
Oh . . . of course, Highness . . . you don't know . . . Müller is the real name of Professor Smith.
That reptile! Where is he? Impale him instantly!
Müller is in the hands of the police, Highness. And I've given my word that he'll have a fair trial.
By Allah! How you Westerners complicate things! . . . We men of the East are far more expeditious!
The trial will attract plenty of attention! . . . I found these papers on him. They prove Müller was a secret agent for a major foreign power . . . In the event of war it was his job to use his men to seize the oil wells, which explains the veritable arsenal we found under his palace . . . And he was already manœuvring to oust Arabex in favour of Skoil.
Those are the essentials. A police search of his palace, and a full interrogation of Müller and his accomplices will fill in the details. Quite simply, it's an episode in the perpetual warfare over oil . . . the world's black gold . . .
Some days later . . .
Tintin! Tintin! . . . A letter from Calculus!
My friends, I have immediately analysed the tablets you sent. I have discovered that if you add only a minute part to petrol its explosive qualities are increased to an alarming degree.
By trial and error I have concluded that one single tablet dissolved in a tank holding 5000 gallons of petrol would be enough to cause a
Anyway, Captain, that solves the mystery of cars blowing up . . . Hey, what's the matter? What have you got there?
Thundering typhoons!

Blistering barnacles! Look at that!

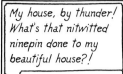

My house, by thunder! What's that nitwitted ninepin done to my beautiful house?!

Let's read on: he's sure to explain . . .

. . . The research was exceedingly difficult. I enclose a photograph of Marlinspike after my first experiments . . .

His first? . . . Did he do some more?!!

. . . Anyway, they were successful: that's all that matters. As for the phenomena in the capillary systems of the Thompsons, these will soon cease with the aid of the powders I have prepared and sent to you separately. The other substance I have sent is for use with petrol, and will entirely neutralize the effects of the compound Formula Fourteen . . .

Some weeks later . . .

"Each day of the Müller trial brings startling new disclosures. Today the whole mystery of the exploding car engines was revealed. It is now known that a major foreign power had developed a new chemical, known simply as Formula Fourteen. This chemical, added to petrol, increased its explosive qualities tenfold . . ."

"In the event of war, the agents of this foreign power could easily contaminate the oil reserves of the other side. The recent outbreak of car explosions was by way of a trial, on a reduced scale, of this new tactic. Thanks to the work of the famous boy reporter, Tintin, the secret of Formula Fourteen has been discovered . . ."

". . . An effective antidote has immediately been developed by his distinguished colleague, Professor Cuthbert Calculus, to neutralize the effects of the chemical. By his prompt action, Tintin has undoubtedly prevented the outbreak of war. Better news too of the detectives Thomson and Thompson who inadvertently swallowed some Formula Fourteen. They are now out of danger, and well on the way to recovery.

What about that? We had a narrow escape, eh? . . . If it hadn't been for the Thompsons, we'd be at war! . . . You know, Captain, you still haven't told us how you came to be mixed up in this business . . .

Oh, yes . . . Well, I . . . thank you, Highness . . .

Well . . . Pff . . . It's like this . . . Pff . . . I think I told you . . . Pff . . . it's quite simple really . . . Pff . . . and at the same time rather complicated . . .

Would you believe it . . . Pff . . . I . . . Pfff . . .

PSHTT

Another of Abdullah's little tricks! . . . And he promised me he'd be good! . . . Ah, what adorable little ways he has!

Adorable! . . . Adorable! . . . I'll say he is!! . . . Well, if you want to hear my story, it won't be from me! . . . Blistering barnacles, as far as I'm concerned, this is the end!

END